Here are seven stran̲ ̲ ̲ ̲ ̲ ̲ ̲ ̲ ̲ ̲ ̲ ̲ ̲ ̲ ̲ ̲ of murder and intrigue, ̲ ̲ ̲ ̲ ̲ ̲ ̲ ̲ ̲g is as it seems and no one can be trusted . . . Why does the young man disguise himself with a false nose? What *are* the unspeakable sins of Prince Saradine? How can an invisible man commit murder?

Father Brown, the unassuming and rather eccentric little priest, becomes entangled in these sensational cases and unfathomable mysteries, and uses his uncanny talents as an amateur detective to unravel the ghastly truth.

G. K. Chesterton was born in London in 1874. At school he showed great literary promise, and while at art school began to review books, an occupation which launched him on his lifelong career as a writer. He wrote on a great variety of topics, but his most famous stories are undoubtedly those of Father Brown, the first of which appeared in 1911. He died in 1936.

G. K. Chesterton

THE PUFFIN
FATHER BROWN
STORIES

PUFFIN BOOKS

PUFFIN BOOKS

Published by the Penguin Group
Penguin Books Ltd, 27 Wrights Lane, London W8 5TZ, England
Viking Penguin, a division of Penguin Books USA Inc.
375 Hudson Street, New York, New York 10014, USA
Penguin Books Australia Ltd, Ringwood, Victoria, Australia
Penguin Books Canada Ltd, 2801 John Street, Markham, Ontario, Canada L3R 1B4
Penguin Books (NZ) Ltd, 182–190 Wairau Road, Auckland 10, New Zealand

Penguin Books Ltd, Registered Offices: Harmondsworth, Middlesex, England

This selection published in Puffin Books 1987
Reprinted 1990

'The Invisible Man' and 'The Sins of Prince
Saradine' first published in *The Innocence
of Father Brown*, 1911; 'The Head of Caesar'
first published in *The Wisdom of Father
Brown*, 1914; 'The Vanishing of Vaudrey',
'The Worst Crime in the World' and 'The Man
with Two Beards' first published in *The
Secret of Father Brown*, 1927; 'The Green
Man' first published in *The Scandal of
Father Brown*, 1935.

Printed and bound in Great Britain by
Cox & Wyman Ltd, Reading

Typeset in Linotron Palatino
by Rowland Phototypesetting Ltd
Bury St Edmunds, Suffolk

CONTENTS

THE HEAD OF CAESAR

There is somewhere in Brompton or Kensington an interminable avenue of tall houses, rich but largely empty, that looks like a terrace of tombs. The very steps up to the dark front doors seem as steep as the side of pyramids; one would hesitate to knock at the door, lest it should be opened by a mummy. But a yet more depressing feature in the grey façade is its telescopic length and changeless continuity. The pilgrim walking down it begins to think he will never come to a break or a corner; but there is one exception – a very small one, but hailed by the pilgrim almost with a shout. There is a sort of mews between two of the tall mansions, a mere slit like the crack of a door by comparison with the street, but just large enough to permit a pygmy alehouse or eating-house, still allowed by the rich to their stable-servants, to stand in the angle. There is something cheery in its very dinginess, and something free and elfin in its very insignificance. At the feet of those grey stone giants it looks like a lighted house of dwarfs.

Anyone passing the place during a certain autumn evening, itself almost fairylike, might have seen a hand pull aside the red half-blind which (along with some large white lettering) half hid the interior from the street, and a face peer out not unlike a rather innocent goblin's. It was, in fact, the face of one with the harmless human name of Brown, formerly priest of Cobhole in Essex, and now working in London. His friend, Flambeau, a semi-official investigator, was sitting opposite him, making his last notes of a case he had cleared up in the neighbourhood. They were sitting at a small table, close up to the window, when the priest pulled the curtain back and looked out. He waited till a stranger in the street had passed the window, to let the curtain fall into its place again. Then his round eyes rolled to the large white lettering on the window above his head, and then strayed to the next table, at which sat only a navvy with beer and cheese, and a young girl with red hair and a glass of milk. Then (seeing his friend put away the pocket-book), he said softly:

'If you've got ten minutes, I wish you'd follow that man with the false nose.'

Flambeau looked up in surprise; but the girl with the red hair also looked up, and with something that was stronger than astonishment. She was simply and even loosely dressed in light brown sacking stuff; but she was a lady, and even, on a second glance, a rather needlessly haughty one: 'The man with the false nose!' repeated Flambeau. 'Who's he?'

'I haven't a notion,' answered Father Brown. 'I want you to find out; I ask it as a favour. He went down there' – and he jerked his thumb over his shoulder in one of his undistinguished gestures – 'and can't have passed three lampposts yet. I only want to know the direction.'

Flambeau gazed at his friend for some time, with an

expression between perplexity and amusement; and then, rising from the table, squeezed his huge form out of the little door of the dwarf tavern, and melted into the twilight.

Father Brown took a small book out of his pocket and began to read steadily; he betrayed no consciousness of the fact that the red-haired lady had left her own table and sat down opposite him. At last she leaned over and said in a low, strong voice: 'Why do you say that? How do you know it's false?'

He lifted his rather heavy eyelids, which fluttered in considerable embarrassment. Then his dubious eye roamed again to the white lettering on the glass front of the public-house. The young woman's eyes followed his, and rested there also, but in pure puzzledom.

'No,' said Father Brown, answering her thoughts. 'It doesn't say "Sela", like the thing in the Psalms; I read it like that myself when I was wool-gathering just now; it says "Ales".'

'Well?' inquired the staring young lady. 'What does it matter what it says?'

His ruminating eye roved to the girl's light canvas sleeve, round the wrist of which ran a very slight thread of artistic pattern, just enough to distinguish it from a working-dress of a common woman and make it more like the working-dress of a lady art-student. He seemed to find much food for thought in this; but his reply was very slow and hesitant. 'You see, madam,' he said, 'from outside the place looks – well, it is a perfectly decent place – but ladies like you don't – don't generally think so. They never go into such places from choice, except –'

'Well?' she repeated.

'Except an unfortunate few who don't go in to drink milk.'

'You are a most singular person,' said the young lady. 'What is your object in all this?'

'Not to trouble you about it,' he replied, very gently. 'Only to arm myself with knowledge enough to help you, if ever you freely ask my help.'

'But why should I need help?'

He continued his dreamy monologue. 'You couldn't have come in to see protégées, humble friends, that sort of thing, or you'd have gone through into the parlour . . . and you couldn't have come in because you were ill, or you'd have spoken to the woman of the place, who's obviously respectable . . . besides, you don't look ill in that way, but only unhappy . . . This street is the only original long lane that has no turning; and the houses on both sides are shut up . . . I could only suppose that you'd seen somebody coming whom you didn't want to meet; and found the public-house was the only shelter in this wilderness of stone . . . I don't think I went beyond the licence of a stranger in glancing at the only man who passed immediately after . . . And as I thought he looked like the wrong sort . . . and you looked like the right sort . . . I held myself ready to help if he annoyed you; that is all. As for my friend, he'll be back soon; and he certainly can't find out anything by stumping down a road like this . . . I didn't think he could.'

'Then why did you send him out?' she cried, leaning forward with yet warmer curiosity. She had the proud, impetuous face that goes with reddish colouring and a Roman nose, as it did in Marie Antoinette.

He looked at her steadily for the first time, and said: 'Because I hoped you would speak to me.'

She looked back at him for some time with a heated face, in which there hung a red shadow of anger; then, despite her anxieties, humour broke out of her eyes and the corners of her mouth, and she answered almost grimly: 'Well, if you're so keen on my conversation, perhaps you'll answer my question.' After a pause she added: 'I had the honour to ask you why you thought the man's nose was false.'

'The wax always spots like that just a little in this weather,' answered Father Brown with entire simplicity.

'But it's such a *crooked* nose,' remonstrated the red-haired girl.

The priest smiled in his turn. 'I don't say it's the sort of nose one would wear out of mere foppery,' he admitted. 'This man, I think, wears it because his real nose is so much nicer.'

'But why?' she insisted.

'What is the nursery rhyme?' observed Brown absent-mindedly. 'There was a crooked man and he went a crooked mile . . . That man, I fancy, has gone a very crooked road – by following his nose.'

'Why, what's he done?' she demanded, rather shakily.

'I don't want to force your confidence by a hair,' said Father Brown, very quietly. 'But I think you could tell me more about that than I can tell you.'

The girl sprang to her feet and stood quite quietly, but with clenched hands, like one about to stride away; then her hands loosened slowly, and she sat down again. 'You are more of a mystery than all the others,' she said desperately; 'but I feel there might be a heart in your mystery.'

'What we all dread most,' said the priest in a low voice, 'is a maze with *no* centre. That is why atheism is only a nightmare.'

'I will tell you everything,' said the red-haired girl doggedly, 'except why I am telling you; and that I don't know.'

She picked at the darned table-cloth and went on: 'You look as if you knew what isn't snobbery as well as what is; and when I say that ours is a good old family, you'll understand it is a necessary part of the story; indeed, my chief danger is in my brother's high and dry notions, *noblesse oblige* and all that. Well, my name is Christabel Carstairs; and my father was that Colonel Carstairs you've probably heard of, who made the famous Carstairs Collection of Roman coins. I could never describe my father to you; the nearest I can say is that he was very like a Roman coin himself. He was as handsome and as genuine and as valuable and as metallic and as out-of-date. He was prouder of his Collection than of his coat of arms – nobody could say more than that. His extraordinary character came out most in his will. He had two sons and one daughter. He quarrelled with one son, my brother Giles, and sent him to Australia on a small allowance. He then made a will leaving the Carstairs Collection, actually with a yet smaller allowance, to my brother Arthur. He meant it as a reward, as the highest honour he could offer, in acknowledgement of Arthur's loyalty and rectitude and the distinctions he had already gained in mathematics and economics at Cambridge. He left me practically all his pretty large fortune; and I am sure he meant it in contempt.

'Arthur, you may say, might well complain of this; but Arthur is my father over again. Though he had some differences with my father in early youth, no sooner had he taken over the Collection than he became like a pagan priest dedicated to a temple. He mixed up these Roman halfpence with the honour of the Carstairs family in the same stiff, idolatrous way as his father before him. He acted as if Roman money must be guarded by all the Roman virtues. He took no pleasures; he spent nothing on himself; he lived for the Collection. Often he would not trouble to dress for his simple meals; but pottered about among the corded brown-paper parcels (which no one else was allowed to touch) in an old brown dressing-gown. With its rope and tassel and his pale, thin, refined face, it made him look like an old ascetic monk. Every now and then, though, he would appear dressed like a decidedly fashionable gentleman; but that was only when he went up to the London sales or shops to make an addition to the Carstairs Collection.

'Now, if you've known any young people, you won't be shocked if I say that I got into rather a low frame of mind with all this; the frame of mind in which one begins to say that the Ancient Romans were all very well in their way. I'm not like my brother Arthur; I can't help enjoying enjoyment. I got a lot of romance and rubbish where I got my red hair, from the other side of the family. Poor Giles was the same; and I think the atmosphere of coins might count in excuse for him; though he really did wrong and nearly went to prison. But he didn't behave any worse than I did; as you shall hear.

'I come now to the silly part of the story. I think a man

as clever as you can guess the sort of thing that would begin to relieve the monotony for an unruly girl of seventeen placed in such a position. But I am so rattled with more dreadful things that I can hardly read my own feeling; and don't know whether I despise it now as a flirtation or bear it as a broken heart. We lived then at a little seaside watering-place in South Wales, and a retired sea-captain living a few doors off had a son about five years older than myself, who had been a friend of Giles before he went to the Colonies. His name does not affect my tale; but I tell you it was Philip Hawker, because I am telling you everything. We used to go shrimping together, and said and thought we were in love with each other; at least he certainly said he was, and I certainly thought I was. If I tell you he had bronzed curly hair and a falconish sort of face, bronzed by the sea also, it's not for his sake, I assure you, but for the story; for it was the cause of a very curious coincidence.

'One summer afternoon, when I had promised to go shrimping along the sands with Philip, I was waiting rather impatiently in the front drawing-room, watching Arthur handle some packets of coins he had just purchased and slowly shunt them, one or two at a time, into his own dark study and museum which was at the back of the house. As soon as I heard the heavy door close on him finally, I made a bolt for my shrimping-net and tam-o'-shanter and was just going to slip out, when I saw that my brother had left behind him one coin that lay gleaming on the long bench by the window. It was a bronze coin, and the colour, combined with the exact curve of the Roman nose and something in the very lift of the long, wiry neck, made the head of Caesar on it the almost precise portrait of Philip Hawker. Then I suddenly remembered Giles telling Philip of a coin that was like him, and Philip wishing he had it. Perhaps you can fancy the wild, foolish thoughts with which my head went round; I felt as if I had had a gift from the fairies. It seemed to me that if I could only run away with this, and give it to Philip like a wild sort of wedding-ring, it would be a bond between us for ever; I felt a thousand such things at once. Then there yawned under me, like the pit, the enormous, awful notion of what I was doing; above all, the unbearable thought, which was like touching hot iron, of what Arthur would think of it. A Carstairs a thief; and a thief of the Carstairs treasure! I believe my brother could see me burned like a witch for such a thing. But then, the very thought of such fanatical cruelty heightened my old hatred of his dingy old antiquarian fussiness and my longing for the youth and liberty that called to me from the sea. Outside was strong sunlight with a wind; and a yellow head of some broom or gorse in the garden rapped against the glass of the window. I thought of that living and growing gold calling to me from all the heaths of the world – and then of that dead, dull gold and bronze and brass of my brother's growing dustier and dustier as life went by. Nature and the Carstairs Collection had come to grips at last.

'Nature is older than the Carstairs Collection. As I ran down the streets to the sea, the coin clenched tight in my fist, I felt all the Roman Empire on my back as well as the Carstairs pedigree. It was not only the old lion argent that was roaring in my ear, but all the eagles of the Caesars seemed flapping and screaming in pursuit of me. And yet my heart rose higher and higher like a child's kite, until I came over the loose, dry sand-hills and to the flat, wet sands, where Philip stood already up to his ankles in the shallow shining water, some hundred yards out to sea. There was a great red sunset; and the long stretch of low water, hardly rising over the ankle for half a mile, was like a lake of ruby flame. It was not till I had torn off my shoes and stockings and waded to where he stood, which was well away from the dry land, that I turned and looked round. We were quite alone in a circle of sea-water and wet sand; and I gave him the head of Caesar.

'At the very instant I had a shock of fancy: that a man far away on the sand-hills was looking at me intently. I must have felt immediately after that it was a mere leap of unreasonable nerves; for the man was only a dark dot in the distance, and I could only just see that he was standing quite still and gazing, with his head a little on one side. There was no earthly logical evidence that he was looking at me; he might have been looking at a ship, or the sunset, or the seagulls, or at any of the people who still strayed here and there on the shore between us. Nevertheless, whatever my start sprang from was prophetic; for, as I gazed, he started walking briskly in a bee-line towards us across the wide wet sands. As he drew nearer and nearer I saw that he was dark and bearded, and that his eyes were marked with dark spectacles. He was dressed poorly but respectably in black, from the old black top hat on his head to the solid black boots on his feet. In spite of these he walked straight into the sea without a flash of hesitation, and came on at me with the steadiness of a travelling bullet.

'I can't tell you the sense of monstrosity and miracle I had when he thus silently burst the barrier between land

and water. It was as if he had walked straight off a cliff and still marched steadily in mid-air. It was as if a house had flown up into the sky or a man's head had fallen off. He was only wetting his boots; but he seemed to be a demon disregarding a law of Nature. If he had hesitated an instant at the water's edge it would have been nothing. As it was, he seemed to look so much at me alone as not to notice the ocean. Philip was some yards away with his back to me, bending over his net. The stranger came on till he stood within two yards of me, the water washing half-way up to his knees. Then he said, with a clearly modulated and rather mincing articulation: "Would it discommode you to contribute elsewhere a coin with a somewhat different superscription?"

'With one exception there was nothing definably abnormal about him. His tinted glasses were not really opaque, but of a blue kind common enough, nor were the eyes behind them shifty, but regarded me steadily. His dark beard was not really long or wild; but he looked rather hairy, because the beard began very high up in his face, just under the cheek-bones. His complexion was neither sallow nor livid, but on the contrary rather clear and youthful; yet this gave a pink-and-white wax look which somehow (I don't know why) rather increased the horror. The only oddity one could fix was that his nose, which was otherwise of a good shape, was just slightly turned sideways at the tip; as if, when it was soft, it had been tapped on one side with a toy hammer. The thing was hardly a deformity; yet I cannot tell you what a living nightmare it was to me. As he stood there in the sunset-stained water he affected me as some hellish sea-monster just risen roaring out of a sea like blood. I don't know why a touch on the nose should affect my imagination so much. I think it seemed as if he could move his nose like a finger. And as if he had just that moment moved it.

'"Any little assistance," he continued with the same queer, priggish accent, "that may obviate the necessity of my communicating with the family."

'Then it rushed over me that I was being blackmailed for the theft of the bronze piece; and all my merely superstitious fears and doubts were swallowed up in one overpowering, practical question. How could he have found out? I had stolen the thing suddenly and on impulse; I was certainly alone; for I always made sure of being unobserved when I slipped out to see Philip in this way. I had not, to all appearance, been followed in the street; and if I had, they could not "X-ray" the coin in my closed hand. The man standing on the sand-hills could no more have seen what I gave Philip than shoot a fly in one eye, like the man in the fairy-tale.

'"Philip," I cried helplessly, "ask this man what he wants."

'When Philip lifted his head at last from mending his net he looked rather red, as if sulky or ashamed; but it may have been only the exertion of stooping and the red evening light; I may have only had another of the morbid fancies that seemed to be dancing about me. He merely said gruffly to the man: "You clear out of this." And, motioning me to follow, set off wading shoreward without paying further attention to him. He stepped on to a stone breakwater that ran out from among the roots of the sand-hills, and so struck homeward, perhaps thinking our incubus would find it less easy to walk on such rough stones, green and slippery with seaweed, than we, who were young and used to it. But my persecutor walked as daintily as he talked; and he still followed me, picking his way and picking his phrases. I heard his delicate, detestable voice appealing to me over my shoulder, until at last, when we had crested the sand-hills, Philip's patience (which was by no means so conspicuous on most occasions) seemed to snap. He turned suddenly, saying, "Go back. I can't talk to you now." And, as the man hovered and opened his mouth, Philip struck him a buffet on it that sent him flying from the top of the tallest sand-hill to the bottom. I saw him crawling out below, covered with sand.

'This stroke comforted me somehow, though it might well increase my peril; but Philip showed none of his usual elation at his own prowess. Though as affectionate as ever, he still seemed cast down; and before I could ask him anything fully, he parted with me at his own gate, with two remarks that struck me as strange. He said that, all things considered, I ought to put the coin back in the Collection; but that he himself would keep it "for the present". And then he added, quite suddenly and irrelevantly: "You know Giles is back from Australia?"'

The door of the tavern opened and the gigantic shadow of the investigator Flambeau fell across the table. Father Brown presented him to the lady in his own slight, persuasive style of speech, mentioning his knowledge and sympathy in such cases; and almost without knowing, the girl was soon reiterating her story to two listeners. But Flambeau, as he bowed and sat down, handed the priest a small slip of paper. Brown accepted it with some surprise and read on it: 'Cab to Wagga Wagga, 379,

Mafeking Avenue, Putney'. The girl was going on with her story.

'I went up the steep street to my own house with my head in a whirl; it had not begun to clear when I came to the doorstep, on which I found a milk-can – and the man with the twisted nose. The milk-can told me the servants were all out; for, of course, Arthur, browsing about in his brown dressing-gown in a brown study, would not hear or answer a bell. Thus there was no one to help me in the house, except my brother, whose help must be my ruin. In desperation I thrust two shillings into the horrid thing's hand, and told him to call again in a few days, when I had thought it out. He went off sulking, but more sheepishly than I had expected – perhaps he had been shaken by his fall – and I watched the star of sand splashed on his back receding down the road with a horrid vindictive pleasure. He turned a corner some six houses down.

'Then I let myself in, made myself some tea, and tried to think it out. I sat at the drawing-room window looking on to the garden, which still glowed with the last full evening light. But I was too distracted and dreamy to look at the lawns and flowerpots and flower-beds with any concentration. So I took the shock the more sharply because I'd seen it so slowly.

'The man or monster I'd sent away was standing quite still in the middle of the garden. Oh, we've all read a lot about pale-faced phantoms in the dark; but this was more dreadful than anything of that kind could ever be. Because, though he cast a long evening shadow, he still stood in warm sunlight. And because his face was not pale, but had that waxen bloom still upon it that belongs to a barber's dummy. He stood quite still, with his face towards me; and I can't tell you how horrid he looked among the tulips and all those tall, gaudy, almost hothouse-looking flowers. It looked as if we'd stuck up a waxwork instead of a statue in the centre of our garden.

'Yet almost the instant he saw me move in the window he turned and ran out of the garden by the back gate, which stood open and by which he had undoubtedly entered. This renewed timidity on his part was so different from the impudence with which he had walked into the sea, that I felt vaguely comforted. I fancied, perhaps, that he feared confronting Arthur more than I knew. Anyhow, I settled down at last, and had a quiet dinner alone (for it was against the rules to disturb Arthur when he was rearranging the museum), and my thoughts, a little released, fled to Philip and lost themselves, I suppose. Anyhow, I was looking blankly, but rather pleasantly than otherwise, at another window, uncurtained, but by this time black as a slate with the final nightfall. It seemed to me that something like a snail was on the outside of the window-pane. But when I stared harder, it was more like a man's thumb pressed on the pane; it had that curled look that a thumb has. With my fear and courage re-awakened together, I rushed at the window and then recoiled with a strangled scream that any man but Arthur must have heard.

'For it was not a thumb, any more than it was a snail. It was the tip of a crooked nose, crushed against the glass; it looked white with the pressure; and the staring face and eyes behind it were at first invisible and afterwards grey like a ghost. I slammed the shutters together somehow, rushed up to my room, and locked myself in. But, even as I passed, I could almost swear I saw a second black window with something on it that was like a snail.

'It might be best to go to Arthur after all. If the thing was crawling close all around the house like a cat, it might have purposes worse even than blackmail. My brother might cast me out and curse me for ever, but he was a gentleman, and would defend me on the spot. After ten minutes' curious thinking, I went down, knocked at the door and then went in: to see the last and worst sight.

'My brother's chair was empty; and he was obviously out. But the man with the crooked nose was sitting waiting for his return, with his hat still insolently on his head, and actually reading one of my brother's books under my brother's lamp. His face was composed and occupied, but his nose-tip still had the air of being the most mobile part of his face, as if it had just turned from left to right like an elephant's proboscis. I had thought him poisonous enough while he was pursuing and watching me; but I think his unconsciousness of my presence was more frightful still.

'I think I screamed loud and long; but that doesn't matter. What I did next does matter: I gave him all the money I had, including a good deal in paper which, though it was mine, I dare say I had no right to touch. He went off at last, with hateful, tactful regrets all in long words; and I sat down, feeling ruined in every sense. And yet I was saved that very night by a pure accident. Arthur had gone off suddenly to London, as he so often did, for bargains; and returned, late but radiant, having nearly secured a treasure that was an added splendour even to the family Collection. He was so resplendent that I was almost emboldened to confess the abstraction of the lesser gem; but he bore down all other topics with his over-powering projects. Because the bargain might still miss fire any moment, he insisted on my packing at once and going up with him to lodgings he had already taken in Fulham, to be near the curio-shop in question. Thus in spite of myself, I fled from my foe almost in the dead of night – but from Philip also . . . My brother was often at the South Kensington Museum, and, in order to make some sort of secondary life for myself, I paid for a few lessons at the Art Schools. I was coming back from them this evening, when I saw the abomination of desolation walking alive down the long straight street and the rest is as this gentleman has said.

'I've got only one thing to say. I don't deserve to be helped; and I don't question or complain of my punish-ment; it is just, it ought to have happened. But I still question, with bursting brains, how it can have hap-pened. Am I punished by miracle? or how *can* anyone but Philip and myself know I gave him a tiny coin in the middle of the sea?'

'It is an extraordinary problem,' admitted Flambeau.

'Not so extraordinary as the answer,' remarked Father Brown, rather gloomily. 'Miss Carstairs, will you be at home if we call at your Fulham place in an hour and a half hence?'

The girl looked at him, and then rose and put her gloves on. 'Yes,' she said, 'I'll be there;' and almost instantly left the place.

That night the detective and the priest were still talking

of the matter as they drew near the Fulham house, a tenement strangely mean even for a temporary residence of the Carstairs family.

'Of course the superficial, on reflection,' said Flambeau, 'would think first of this Australian brother who's been in trouble before, who's come back so suddenly and who's just the man to have shabby confederates. But I can't see how he can come into the thing by any process of thought, unless –'

'Well?' asked his companion patiently.

Flambeau lowered his voice. 'Unless the girl's lover comes in, too, and he would be the blacker villain. The Australian chap did know that Hawker wanted the coin. But I can't see how on earth he could know that Hawker had got it, unless Hawker signalled to him or his representative across the shore.'

'That is true,' assented the priest, with respect.

'Have you noted another thing?' went on Flambeau eagerly; 'this Hawker hears his love insulted, but doesn't strike till *he's got to the soft sand-hills*, where he can be victor in a mere sham-fight. If he'd struck amid rocks and sea, he might have hurt his ally.'

'That is true again,' said Father Brown, nodding.

'And now, take it from the start. It lies between few people, but at least three. You want one person for suicide; two people for murder; but at least three people for blackmail.'

'Why?' asked the priest softly.

'Well, obviously,' cried his friend, 'there must be one to be exposed; one to threaten exposure; and one at least whom exposure would horrify.'

After a long ruminant pause, the priest said: 'You miss

a logical step. Three persons are needed as ideas. Only two are needed as agents.'

'What can you mean?' asked the other.

'Why shouldn't a blackmailer,' asked Brown, in a low voice, 'threaten his victim with himself? Suppose a wife became a rigid teetotaller *in order* to frighten her husband into concealing *his* pub-frequenting, and then wrote him blackmailing letters in another hand, threatening to tell his wife! Why shouldn't it work? Suppose a father forbade a son to gamble, and then, following him in a good disguise, threatened the boy with his own sham paternal strictness! Suppose – but here we are, my friend.'

'My God!' cried Flambeau; 'you don't mean –'

An active figure ran down the steps of the house and showed under the golden lamplight the unmistakable head that resembled the Roman coin. 'Miss Carstairs,' said Hawker without ceremony, 'wouldn't go in till you came.'

'Well,' observed Brown confidentially, 'don't you think it's the best thing she can do to stop outside – with you to look after her? You see, I rather guess you have guessed it all yourself.'

'Yes,' said the young man, in an undertone, 'I guessed on the sands and now I know; that was why I let him fall soft.'

Taking a latchkey from the girl and the coin from Hawker, Flambeau let himself and his friend into the empty house and passed into the outer parlour. It was empty of all occupants but one. The man whom Father Brown had seen pass the tavern was standing against the wall as if at bay; unchanged, save that he had taken off his black coat and was wearing a brown dressing-gown.

'We have come,' said Father Brown politely, 'to give back this coin to its owner.' And he handed it to the man with the nose.

Flambeau's eyes rolled. 'Is this man a coin-collector?' he asked.

'This man is Mr Arthur Carstairs,' said the priest positively, 'and he is a coin-collector of a somewhat singular kind.'

The man changed colour so horribly that the crooked nose stood out on his face like a separate and comic thing. He spoke, nevertheless, with a sort of despairing dignity. 'You shall see, then,' he said, 'that I have not lost all the family qualities.' And he turned suddenly and strode into an inner room, slamming the door.

'Stop him!' shouted Father Brown, bounding and half falling over a chair; and, after a wrench or two, Flambeau had the door open. But it was too late. In dead silence Flambeau strode across and telephoned for doctor and police.

An empty medicine bottle lay on the floor. Across the table the body of the man in the brown dressing-gown lay amid his burst and gaping brown-paper parcels; out of which poured and rolled, not Roman, but very modern English coins.

The priest held up the bronze head of Caesar. 'This,' he said, 'was all that was left of the Carstairs Collection.'

After a silence he went on, with more than common gentleness: 'It was a cruel will his wicked father made, and you see he did resent it a little. He hated the Roman money he had, and grew fonder of the real money denied him. He not only sold the Collection bit by bit, but sank bit by bit to the basest ways of making money – even to blackmailing his own family in a disguise. He black-mailed his brother from Australia for his little forgotten crime (that is why he took the cab to Wagga Wagga in Putney), he blackmailed his sister for the theft he alone could have noticed. And that, by the way, is why she had that supernatural guess when he was away on the sand-dunes. Mere figure and gait, however distant, are more likely to remind us of somebody than a well-made-up face quite close.'

There was another silence. 'Well,' growled the detective, 'and so this great numismatist and coin-collector was nothing but a vulgar miser.'

'Is there so great a difference?' asked Father Brown, in the same strange, indulgent tone. 'What is there wrong about a miser that is not often as wrong about a collector? What is wrong, except . . . thou shalt not make to thyself any graven image; thou shalt not bow down to them nor serve them, for I . . . but we must go and see how the poor young people are getting on.'

'I think,' said Flambeau, 'that, in spite of everything, they are probably getting on very well.'

THE INVISIBLE MAN

In the cool blue twilight of two steep streets in Camden Town, the shop at the corner, a confectioner's, glowed like the butt of a cigar. One should rather say, perhaps, like the butt of a firework, for the light was of many colours and some complexity, broken up by many mirrors and dancing on many gilt and gaily-coloured cakes and sweetmeats. Against this one fiery glass were glued the noses of many guttersnipes, for the chocolates were all wrapped in those red and gold and green metallic colours which are almost better than chocolate itself; and the huge white wedding-cake in the window was somehow at once remote and satisfying, just as if the whole North Pole were good to eat. Such rainbow provocations could naturally collect the youth of the neighbourhood up to the ages of ten or twelve. But this corner was also attractive to youth at a later stage; and a young man, not less than twenty-four, was staring into the same shop-window. To him, also, the shop was of fiery charm, but this attraction was not wholly to be explained by chocolates; which, however, he was far from despising.

He was a tall, burly, red-haired young man, with a resolute face but a listless manner. He carried under his arm a flat, grey portfolio of black-and-white sketches which he had sold with more or less success to publishers ever since his uncle (who was an admiral) had disinherited him for Socialism, because of a lecture which he had delivered against that economic theory. His name was John Turnbull Angus.

Entering at last, he walked through the confectioner's shop into the back room, which was a sort of pastry-cook restaurant, merely raising his hat to the young lady who was serving there. She was a dark, elegant, alert girl in black, with a high colour and very quick, dark eyes; and after the ordinary interval she followed him into the inner room to take his order.

His order was evidently a usual one. 'I want, please,' he said with precision, 'one halfpenny bun and a small cup of black coffee.' An instant before the girl could turn away he added, 'Also, I want you to marry me.'

The young lady of the shop stiffened suddenly, and said: 'Those are jokes I don't allow.'

The red-haired young man lifted grey eyes of an unexpected gravity.

'Really and truly,' he said, 'it's as serious – as serious as the halfpenny bun. It is expensive, like the bun; one pays for it. It is indigestible, like the bun. It hurts.'

The dark young lady had never taken her dark eyes off him, but seemed to be studying him with almost tragic exactitude. At the end of her scrutiny she had something like the shadow of a smile, and she sat down in a chair.

'Don't you think,' observed Angus, absently, 'that it's rather cruel to eat these halfpenny buns? They might grow up into penny buns. I shall give up these brutal sports when we are married.'

The dark young lady rose from her chair and walked to the window, evidently in a state of strong but not unsympathetic cogitation. When at last she swung round again with an air of resolution, she was bewildered to observe that the young man was carefully laying out on the table various objects from the shop-window. They included a pyramid of highly coloured sweets, several plates of sandwiches, and the two decanters containing that mysterious port and sherry which are peculiar to pastry-cooks. In the middle of this neat arrangement he had carefully let down the enormous load of white sugared cake which had been the huge ornament of the window.

'What on earth are you doing?' she asked.

'Duty, my dear Laura,' he began.

'Oh, for the Lord's sake, stop a minute,' she cried, 'and don't talk to me in that way. I mean what is all that?'

'A ceremonial meal, Miss Hope.'

'And what is *that*?' she asked impatiently, pointing to the mountain of sugar.

'The wedding-cake, Mrs Angus,' he said.

The girl marched to that article, removed it with some clatter, and put it back in the shop-window; she then returned, and, putting her elegant elbows on the table, regarded the young man not unfavourably, but with considerable exasperation.

'You don't give me any time to think,' she said.

'I'm not such a fool,' he answered; 'that's my Christian humility.'

She was still looking at him; but she had grown considerably graver behind the smile.

'Mr Angus,' she said steadily, 'before there is a minute

more of this nonsense I must tell you something about myself as shortly as I can.'

'Delighted,' replied Angus gravely. 'You might tell me something about myself, too, while you are about it.'

'Oh, do hold your tongue and listen,' she said. 'It's nothing that I'm ashamed of, and it isn't even anything that I'm specially sorry about. But what would you say if there were something that is no business of mine and yet is my nightmare?'

'In that case,' said the man seriously, 'I should suggest that you bring back the cake.'

'Well, you must listen to the story first,' said Laura, persistently. 'To begin with, I must tell you that my father owned the inn called the Red Fish at Ludbury, and I used to serve people in the bar.'

'I have often wondered,' he said, 'why there was a kind of a Christian air about this one confectioner's shop.'

'Ludbury is a sleepy, grassy little hole in the Eastern Counties, and the only kind of people who ever came to the Red Fish were occasional commercial travellers, and for the rest, the most awful people you can see, only you've never seen them. I mean little, loungy men, who had just enough to live on, and had nothing to do but lean about in bar-rooms and bet on horses, in bad clothes that were just too good for them. Even these wretched young rotters were not very common at our house; but there were two of them that were a lot too common – common in every sort of way. They both lived on money of their own, and were wearisomely idle and over-dressed. But yet I was a bit sorry for them, because I half believe they slunk into our little empty bar because each of them had a slight deformity; the sort of thing that some yokels laugh at. It wasn't exactly a deformity either; it was more an oddity. One of them was a surprisingly small man, something like a dwarf, or at least like a jockey. He was not at all jockeyish to look at, though; he had a round black head and a well-trimmed black beard, bright eyes like a bird's; he jingled money in his pockets; he jangled a great gold watch-chain; and he never turned up except dressed just too much like a gentleman to be one. He was no fool, though, though a futile idler; he was curiously clever at all kinds of things that couldn't be the slightest use; a sort of impromptu conjuring; making fifteen matches set fire to each other like a regular firework; or cutting a banana or some such thing into a dancing doll. His name was Isidore Smythe; and I can see him still, with his little dark face, just coming up to the counter, making a jumping kangaroo out of five cigars.

'The other fellow was more silent and more ordinary; but somehow he alarmed me much more than poor little Smythe. He was very tall and slight, and light-haired; his nose had a high bridge, and he might almost have been handsome in a spectral sort of way; but he had one of the most appalling squints I have ever seen or heard of. When he looked straight at you, you didn't know where you were yourself, let alone what he was looking at. I fancy this sort of disfigurement embittered the poor chap a little; for while Smythe was ready to show off his monkey tricks anywhere, James Welkin (that was the squinting man's name) never did anything except soak in our bar parlour, and go for great walks by himself in the flat, grey country all round. All the same, I think Smythe, too, was a little sensitive about being so small, though he carried it off more smartly. And so it was that I was really puzzled, as well as startled, and very sorry, when they both offered to marry me in the same week.

'Well, I did what I've since thought was perhaps a silly thing. But, after all, these freaks were my friends in a way; and I had a horror of their thinking I refused them for the real reason, which was that they were so impossibly ugly. So I made up some gas of another sort, about never meaning to marry anyone who hadn't carved his way in the world. I said it was a point of principle with me not to live on money that was just inherited like theirs. Two days after I had talked in this well-meaning sort of way, the whole trouble began. The first thing I heard was that both of them had gone off to seek their fortunes, as if they were in some silly fairy-tale.

'Well, I've never seen either of them from that day to this. But I've had two letters from the little man called Smythe, and really they were rather exciting.'

'Ever heard of the other man?' asked Angus.

'No, he never wrote,' said the girl, after an instant's hesitation. 'Smythe's first letter was simply to say that he had started out walking with Welkin to London; but Welkin was such a good walker that the little man dropped out of it, and took a rest by the roadside. He happened to be picked up by some travelling show, and, partly because he was nearly a dwarf, and partly because he was really a clever little wretch, he got on quite well in the show business, and was soon sent up to the Aquarium, to do some tricks that I forgot. That was his first letter. His second was much more of a startler, and I only got it last week.'

The man called Angus emptied his coffee-cup and

regarded her with mild and patient eyes. Her own mouth took a slight twist of laughter as she resumed: 'I suppose you've seen on the hoardings all about this "Smythe's Silent Service"? Or you must be the only person that hasn't. Oh, I don't know much about it, it's some clockwork invention for doing all the housework by machinery. You know the sort of thing: "Press a button – A Butler who Never Drinks". "Turn a handle – Ten House-maids who Never Flirt". You must have seen the advertisements. Well, whatever these machines are, they are making pots of money; and they are making it all for that little imp whom I knew down in Ludbury. I can't help feeling pleased the poor little chap has fallen on his feet; but the plain fact is, I'm in terror of his turning up any minute and telling me he's carved his way in the world – as he certainly has.'

'And the other man?' repeated Angus with a sort of obstinate quietude.

Laura Hope got to her feet suddenly. 'My friend,' she said: 'I think you are a witch. Yes, you are quite right. I have not seen a line of the other man's writing; and I have no more notion than the dead of what or where he is. But it is of him that I am frightened. It is he who is all about my path. It is he who has half driven me mad. Indeed, I think he has driven me mad; for I have felt him where he could not have been, and I have heard his voice when he could not have spoken.'

'Well, my dear,' said the young man, cheerfully, 'if he were Satan himself, he is done for now you have told somebody. One goes mad all alone, old girl. But when was it you fancied you felt and heard our squinting friend?'

'I heard James Welkin laugh as plainly as I hear you speak,' said the girl, steadily. 'There was nobody there, for I stood just outside the shop at the corner, and could see down both streets at once. I had forgotten how he laughed, though his laugh was as odd as his squint. I had not thought of him for nearly a year. But it's a solemn truth that a few seconds later the first letter came from his rival.'

'Did you ever make the spectre speak or squeak, or anything?' asked Angus, with some interest.

Laura suddenly shuddered, and then said with an unshaken voice: 'Yes. Just when I had finished reading the second letter from Isidore Smythe announcing his success, just then, I heard Welkin say: "He shan't have you, though." It was quite plain, as if he were in the room. It is awful; I think I must be mad.'

'If you really were mad,' said the young man, 'you would think you must be sane. But certainly there seems to me to be something a little rum about this unseen gentleman. Two heads are better than one – I spare you allusions to any other organs – and really, if you would allow me, as a sturdy, practical man, to bring back the wedding-cake out of the window –'

Even as he spoke, there was a sort of steely shriek in the street outside, and a small motor, driven at devilish speed, shot up to the door of the shop and stuck there. In the same flash of time a small man in a shiny top hat stood stamping in the outer room.

Angus, who had hitherto maintained hilarious ease from motives of mental hygiene, revealed the strain of his soul by striding abruptly out of the inner room and confronting the newcomer. A glance at him was quite sufficient to confirm the savage guesswork of a man in love. This very dapper but dwarfish figure, with the spike of black beard carried insolently forward, the clever unrestful eyes, the neat but very nervous fingers, could be none other than the man just described to him: Isidore Smythe, who made dolls out of banana skins and match-boxes: Isidore Smythe, who made millions out of un-drinking butlers and unflirting housemaids of metal. For a moment the two men, instinctively understanding each other's air of possession, looked at each other with that curious cold generosity which is the soul of rivalry.

Mr Smythe, however, made no allusion to the ultimate ground of their antagonism, but said simply and explo-sively: 'Has Miss Hope seen that thing on the window?'

'On the window?' repeated the staring Angus.

'There's no time to explain other things,' said the small millionaire shortly. 'There's some tomfoolery going on here that has to be investigated.'

He pointed his polished walking-stick at the window, recently depleted by the bridal preparations of Mr Angus; and that gentleman was astonished to see along the front of the glass a long strip of paper pasted, which had certainly not been on the window when he had looked through it some time before. Following the energetic Smythe outside into the street, he found that some yard and a half of stamp paper had been carefully gummed along the glass outside, and on this was written in straggly characters: 'If you marry Smythe, he will die.'

'Laura,' said Angus, putting his big red head into the shop, 'you're not mad.'

'It's the writing of that fellow Welkin,' said Smythe

gruffly. 'I haven't seen him for years, but he's always bothering me. Five times in the last fortnight he's had threatening letters left at my flat, and I can't even find out who leaves them, let alone if it is Welkin himself. The porter of the flats swears that no suspicious characters have been seen, and here he has pasted up a sort of dado on a public shop-window, while the people in the shop –'

'Quite so,' said Angus modestly, 'while the people in the shop were having tea. Well, sir, I can assure you I appreciate your common sense in dealing so directly with the matter. We can talk about other things afterwards. The fellow cannot be very far off yet, for I swear there was no paper there when I went last to the window, ten or fifteen minutes ago. On the other hand, he's too far off to be chased, as we don't even know the direction. If you'll take my advice, Mr Smythe, you'll put this at once in the hands of some energetic inquiry man, private rather than public. I know an extremely clever fellow, who has set up in business five minutes from here in your car. His name's Flambeau, and though his youth was a bit stormy, he's a strictly honest man now, and his brains are worth money. He lives in Lucknow Mansions, Hampstead.'

'That is odd,' said the little man, arching his black eyebrows. 'I live myself in Himalaya Mansions round the corner. Perhaps you might care to come with me; I can go to my rooms and sort out these queer Welkin documents, while you run round and get your friend the detective.'

'You are very good,' said Angus politely. 'Well, the sooner we act the better.'

Both men, with a queer kind of impromptu fairness,

took the same sort of formal farewell of the lady, and both jumped into the brisk little car. As Smythe took the wheel and they turned the great corner of the street, Angus was amused to see a gigantesque poster of 'Smythe's Silent Service', with a picture of a huge headless iron doll, carrying a saucepan with the legend, 'A Cook Who is Never Cross'.

'I use them in my own flat,' said the little black-bearded man, laughing, 'partly for advertisement, and partly for real convenience. Honestly, and all above board, those big clockwork dolls of mine do bring you coals or claret or a timetable quicker than any live servants I've ever known, if you know which knob to press. But I'll never deny, between ourselves, that such servants have their disadvantages, too.'

'Indeed?' said Angus; 'is there something they can't do?'

'Yes,' replied Smythe coolly; 'they can't tell me who left those threatening letters at my flat.'

The man's motor was small and swift like himself; in fact, like his domestic service, it was of his own invention. If he was an advertising quack, he was one who believed in his own wares. The sense of something tiny and flying was accentuated as they swept up long white curves of road in the dead but open daylight of evening. Soon the white curves came sharper and dizzier; they were upon ascending spirals, as they say in the modern religions. For, indeed, they were cresting a corner of London which is almost as precipitous as Edinburgh, if not quite so picturesque. Terrace rose above terrace, and the special tower of flats they sought rose above them all to almost Egyptian height, gilt by the level sunset. The change, as they turned the corner and entered the crescent known as Himalaya Mansions, was as abrupt as the opening of a window; for they found that pile of flats sitting above London as above a green sea of slate. Opposite to the mansions, on the other side of the gravel crescent, was a bushy enclosure more like a steep hedge or dyke than a garden, and some way below that ran a strip of artificial water, a sort of canal, like the moat of that embowered fortress. As the car swept round the crescent it passed, at one corner, the stray stall of a man selling chestnuts; and right away at the other end of the curve, Angus could see a dim blue policeman walking slowly. These were the only human shapes in that high suburban solitude; but he had an irrational sense that they expressed the speechless poetry of London. He felt as if they were figures in a story.

The little car shot up to the right house like a bullet, and shot out its owner like a bombshell. He was immediately inquiring of a tall commissionaire in shining braid, and a short porter in shirt-sleeves, whether anybody or anything had been seeking his apartments. He was assured that nobody and nothing had passed these officials since his last inquiries; whereupon he and the slightly bewildered Angus were shot up in the lift like a rocket, till they reached the top floor.

'Just come in for a minute,' said the breathless Smythe. 'I want to show you those Welkin letters. Then you might run round the corner and fetch your friend.' He pressed a button concealed in the wall, and the door opened of itself.

It opened on a long, commodious ante-room, of which the only arresting features, ordinarily speaking, were the rows of tall half-human mechanical figures that stood up on both sides like tailors' dummies. Like tailors' dummies they were headless; and like tailors' dummies they had a handsome unnecessary humpiness in the shoulders, and a pigeon-breasted protuberance of chest; but barring this, they were not much more like a human figure than any automatic machine at a station that is about the human height. They had two great hooks like arms, for carrying trays; and they were painted pea-green, or vermilion, or black for convenience of distinction; in every other way they were only automatic machines and nobody would have looked twice at them. On this occasion, at least, nobody did. For between the two rows of these domestic dummies lay something more interesting than most of the mechanics of the world. It was a white, tattered scrap of paper scrawled with red ink; and the agile inventor had snatched it up almost as soon as the door flew open. He handed it to Angus without a word. The red ink on it actually was not dry, and the message ran: 'If you have been to see her today, I shall kill you.'

There was a short silence, and then Isidore Smythe said quietly: 'Would you like a little whisky: I rather feel as if I should.'

'Thank you; I should like a little Flambeau,' said Angus, gloomily. 'This business seems to me to be getting rather grave. I'm going round at once to fetch him.'

'Right you are,' said the other, with admirable cheerfulness. 'Bring him round here as quick as you can.'

But as Angus closed the front door behind him he saw Smythe push back a button, and one of the clockwork images glided from its place and slid along a groove in the floor carrying a tray with syphon and decanter. There did seem something a trifle weird about leaving the little man alone among those dead servants, who were coming to life as the door closed.

Six steps down from Smythe's landing the man in shirt-sleeves was doing something with a pail. Angus stopped to extract a promise, fortified with a prospective bribe, that he would remain in that place until the return with the detective, and would keep count of any kind of stranger coming up those stairs. Dashing down to the front hall he then laid similar charges of vigilance on the commissionaire at the front door, from whom he learned the simplifying circumstance that there was no back door. Not content with this, he captured the floating policeman and induced him to stand opposite the entrance and watch it; and finally paused an instant for a pennyworth of chestnuts, and an inquiry as to the probable length of the merchant's stay in the neighbourhood.

The chestnut seller, turning up the collar of his coat, told him he should probably be moving shortly, as he thought it was going to snow. Indeed, the evening was growing grey and bitter, but Angus, with all his eloquence, proceeded to nail the chestnut man to his post.

'Keep yourself warm on your own chestnuts,' he said earnestly. 'Eat up your whole stock; I'll make it worth your while. I'll give you a sovereign if you'll wait here till I come back, and then tell me whether any man, woman, or child has gone into that house where the commissionaire is standing.'

He then walked away smartly, with a last look at the besieged tower.

'I've made a ring round that room, anyhow,' he said. 'They can't all four of them be Mr Welkin's accomplices.'

Lucknow Mansions were, so to speak, on a lower platform of that hill of houses, of which Himalaya Mansions might be called the peak. Mr Flambeau's semi-official flat was on the ground floor, and presented in every way a marked contrast to the American machinery and cold hotel-like luxury of the flat of the Silent Service. Flambeau, who was a friend of Angus, received him in a rococo artistic den behind his office, of which the ornaments were sabres, harquebuses, Eastern curiosities, flasks of Italian wine, savage cooking-pots, a plumy Persian cat, and a small dusty-looking Roman Catholic priest, who looked particularly out of place.

'This is my friend, Father Brown,' said Flambeau. 'I've often wanted you to meet him. Splendid weather, this; a little cold for Southerners like me.'

'Yes, I think it will keep clear,' said Angus, sitting down on a violet-striped Eastern ottoman.

'No,' said the priest quietly; 'it has begun to snow.'

And indeed, as he spoke, the first few flakes, foreseen by the man of chestnuts, began to drift across the darkening window-pane.

'Well,' said Angus heavily. 'I'm afraid I've come on business, and rather jumpy business at that. The fact is, Flambeau, within a stone's throw of your house is a fellow who badly wants your help; he's perpetually being haunted and threatened by an invisible enemy – a scoundrel whom nobody has even seen.' As Angus proceeded to tell the whole tale of Smythe and Welkin beginning with Laura's story, and going on with his own, the supernatural laugh at the corner of two empty streets, the strange distinct words spoken in an empty room, Flambeau grew more and more vividly concerned, and the little priest seemed to be left out of it, like a piece of furniture. When it came to the scribbled stamp-paper pasted on the window, Flambeau rose, seeming to fill the room with his huge shoulders.

'If you don't mind,' he said, 'I think you had better tell me the rest on the nearest road to this man's house. It strikes me, somehow, that there is no time to be lost.'

'Delighted,' said Angus, rising also, 'though he's safe enough for the present, for I've set four men to watch the only hole to his burrow.'

They turned out into the street, the small priest trundling after them with the docility of a small dog. He merely said, in a cheerful way, like one making conversation: 'How quick the snow gets thick on the ground.'

As they threaded the steep side streets already powdered with silver, Angus finished his story; and by the time they reached the crescent with the towering flats, he had leisure to turn his attention to the four sentinels. The chestnut seller, both before and after receiving a sovereign, swore stubbornly that he had watched the door and seen no visitor enter. The policeman was even more emphatic. He said he had had experience of crooks of all kinds, in top hats and in rags; he wasn't so green as to expect suspicious characters to look suspicious; he looked out for anybody, and, so help him, there had been nobody. And when all three men gathered round the gilded commissionaire, who still stood smiling astride of the porch, the verdict was more final still.

'I've got a right to ask any man, duke or dustman, what he wants in these flats,' said the genial and gold-laced giant, 'and I'll swear there's been nobody to ask since this gentleman went away.'

The unimportant Father Brown, who stood back, looking modestly at the pavement, here ventured to say meekly: 'Has nobody been up and down stairs, then, since the snow began to fall? It began while we were all round at Flambeau's.'

'Nobody's been in here, sir, you can take it from me,' said the official, with beaming authority.

'Then I wonder what that is?' said the priest, and stared at the ground blankly like a fish.

The others all looked down also; and Flambeau used a fierce exclamation and a French gesture. For it was unquestionably true that down the middle of the entrance guarded by the man in gold lace, actually between the arrogant, stretched legs of that colossus, ran a stringy pattern of grey footprints stamped upon the white snow.

'God!' cried Angus involuntarily; 'the Invisible Man!'

Without another word he turned and dashed up the stairs, with Flambeau following; but Father Brown still stood looking about him in the snow-clad street as if he had lost interest in his query.

Flambeau was plainly in a mood to break down the door with his big shoulder; but the Scotsman, with more reason, if less intuition, fumbled about on the frame of the door till he found the invisible button; and the door swung slowly open.

It showed substantially the same serried interior; the hall had grown darker, though it was still struck here and there with the last crimson shafts of sunset, and one or two of the headless machines had been moved from their places for this or that purpose, and stood here and there about the twilit place. The green and red of their coats were all darkened in the dusk, and their likeness to human shapes slightly increased by their very shapelessness. But in the middle of them all, exactly where the paper with the red ink had lain, there lay something that looked very like red ink spilled out of its bottle. But it was not red ink.

With a French combination of reason and violence Flambeau simply said 'Murder!' and, plunging into the flat, had explored every corner and cupboard of it in five minutes. But if he expected to find a corpse he found none. Isidore Smythe simply was not in the place, either dead or alive. After the most tearing search the two men met each other in the outer hall with streaming faces and staring eyes. 'My friend,' said Flambeau, talking French in his excitement, 'not only is your murderer invisible, but he makes invisible also the murdered man.'

Angus looked round at the dim room full of dummies, and in some Celtic corner of his Scotch soul a shudder started. One of the life-size dolls stood immediately overshadowing the bloodstain, summoned, perhaps, by the slain man an instant before he fell. One of the high-shouldered hooks that served the thing for arms was a little lifted and Angus had suddenly the horrid fancy that poor Smythe's own iron child had struck him down. Matter had rebelled, and these machines had killed their master. But even so, what had they done with him?

'Eaten him?' said the nightmare at his ear; and he sickened for an instant at the idea of rent, human remains absorbed and crushed into all that acephalous clockwork.

He recovered his mental health by an emphatic effort, and said to Flambeau: 'Well, there it is. The poor fellow has evaporated like a cloud and left a red streak on the floor. The tale does not belong to this world.'

'There is only one thing to be done,' said Flambeau, 'whether it belongs to this world or the other, I must go down and talk to my friend.'

They descended, passing the man with the pail, who again asseverated that he had let no intruder pass, down to the commissionaire and the hovering chestnut man, who rightly reasserted their own watchfulness. But when Angus looked round for his fourth confirmation he could not see it, and called out with some nervousness: 'Where is the policeman?'

'I beg your pardon,' said Father Brown; 'that is my fault. I just sent him down the road to investigate something – that I just thought worth investigating.'

'Well, we want him back pretty soon,' said Angus abruptly, 'for the wretched man upstairs has not only been murdered, but wiped out.'

'How?' asked the priest.

'Father,' said Flambeau, after a pause, 'upon my soul I believe it is more in your department than mine. No friend or foe has entered the house, but Smythe is gone, as if stolen by the fairies. If that is not supernatural, I –'

As he spoke they were all checked by an unusual sight; the big blue policeman came round the corner of the crescent running. He came straight up to Brown.

'You're right, sir,' he panted, 'they've just found poor Mr Smythe's body in the canal down below.'

Angus put his hand wildly to his head. 'Did he run down and drown himself?' he asked.

'He never came down, I'll swear,' said the constable, 'and he wasn't drowned either, for he died of a great stab over the heart.'

'And yet you saw no one enter?' said Flambeau in a grave voice.

'Let us walk down the road a little,' said the priest.

As they reached the other end of the crescent he observed abruptly: 'Stupid of me! I forgot to ask the policeman something. I wonder if they found a light brown sack.'

'Why a light brown sack?' asked Angus, astonished.

'Because if it was any other coloured sack, the case must begin over again,' said Father Brown; 'but if it was a light brown sack, why, the case is finished.'

'I am pleased to hear it,' said Angus with hearty irony. 'It hasn't begun, so far as I am concerned.'

'You must tell us all about it,' said Flambeau, with a strange heavy simplicity, like a child.

Unconsciously they were walking with quickening steps down the long sweep of road on the other side of the high crescent, Father Brown leading briskly, though in silence. At last he said with an almost touching vagueness: 'Well, I'm afraid you'll think it so prosy. We always begin at the abstract end of things, and you can't begin this story anywhere else.

'Have you ever noticed this – that people never answer what you say? They answer what you mean – or what they think you mean. Suppose one lady says to another in a country house, "Is anybody staying with you?" the lady doesn't answer "Yes; the butler, the three footmen, the parlourmaid, and so on," though the parlourmaid may be in the room, or the butler behind her chair. She says: "There is *nobody* staying with us," meaning nobody of the sort you mean. But suppose a doctor inquiring into an epidemic asks, "Who is staying in the house?" then the lady will remember the butler, the parlourmaid, and the rest. All language is used like that; you never get a question answered literally, even when you get it answered truly. When those four quite honest men said that no man had gone into the mansions, they did not really mean that *no man* had gone into them. They meant no man whom they could suspect of being your man. A man did go into the house, and did come out of it, but they never noticed him.'

'An invisible man?' inquired Angus, raising his red eyebrows.

'A mentally invisible man,' said Father Brown.

A minute or two after he resumed in the same unassuming voice, like a man thinking his way. 'Of course, you can't think of such a man, until you do think of him. That's where his cleverness comes in. But I came to think of him through two or three little things in the tale Mr Angus told us. First, there was the fact that this Welkin went for long walks. And then there was the vast lot of stamp paper on the window. And then, most of all, there were the two things the young lady said – things that couldn't be true. Don't get annoyed,' he added hastily, noting a sudden movement of the Scotsman's head; 'she thought they were true all right, but they couldn't be true. A person *can't* be quite alone in a street a second before she receives a letter. She can't be quite alone in a street when she starts reading a letter just received. There must be somebody pretty near her; he must be mentally invisible.'

'Why must there be somebody near her?' asked Angus.

'Because,' said Father Brown: 'barring carrier-pigeons, somebody must have brought her the letter.'

'Do you really mean to say,' asked Flambeau, with energy, 'that Welkin carried his rival's letters to his lady?'

'Yes,' said the priest. 'Welkin carried his rival's letters to his lady. You see, he had to.'

'Oh, I can't stand much more of this,' exploded Flambeau. 'Who is this fellow? What does he look like? What is the usual get-up of a mentally invisible man?'

'He is dressed rather handsomely in red, blue and gold,' replied the priest promptly with decision, 'and in this striking, and even showy costume he entered Himalaya Mansions under eight human eyes; he killed Smythe in cold blood, and came down into the street again carrying the dead body in his arms –'

'Reverend sir,' cried Angus, standing still, 'are you raving mad, or am I?'

'You are not mad,' said Brown, 'only a little unobservant. You have not noticed such a man as this, for example.'

He took three quick strides forward, and put his hand on the shoulder of an ordinary passing postman who had bustled by them unnoticed under the shade of the trees.

'Nobody ever notices postmen, somehow,' he said thoughtfully; 'yet they have passions like other men, and even carry large bags where a small corpse can be stowed quite easily.'

The postman, instead of turning naturally, had ducked and tumbled against the garden fence. He was a lean fair-bearded man of very ordinary appearance, but as he turned an alarmed face over his shoulder, all three men were fixed with an almost fiendish squint.

Flambeau went back to his sabres, purple rugs and Persian cat, having many things to attend to. John Turnbull Angus went back to the lady at the shop, with whom that imprudent young man contrives to be extremely comfortable. But Father Brown walked these snow-covered hills under the stars for many hours with a murderer, and what they said to each other will never be known.

THE VANISHING OF VAUDREY

Sir Arthur Vaudrey, in his light-grey summer suit, and wearing on his grey head the white hat which he so boldly affected, went walking briskly up the road by the river from his own house to the little group of houses that were almost like outhouses to his own, entered that little hamlet, and then vanished completely as if he had been carried away by the fairies.

The disappearance seemed the more absolute and abrupt because of the familiarity of the scene and the extreme simplicity of the conditions of the problem. The hamlet could not be called a village; indeed, it was little more than a small and strangely isolated street. It stood in the middle of wide and open fields and plains, a mere string of the four or five shops absolutely needed by the neighbours; that is, by a few farmers and the family at the great house. There was a butcher's at the corner, at which, it appeared, Sir Arthur had last been seen. He was seen by two young men staying at his house – Evan Smith, who was acting as his secretary, and John Dalmon, who was generally supposed to be engaged to his ward. There was next to the butcher's a small shop combining a large number of functions, such as is found in villages, in which a little old woman sold sweets, walking-sticks, golf balls, gum, balls of string and a very faded sort of stationery. Beyond this was the tobacconist, to which the two young men were betaking themselves when they last caught a glimpse of their host standing in front of the butcher's shop; and beyond that was a dingy little dressmaker's, kept by two ladies. A pale and shiny shop, offering to the passer-by great goblets of very wan, green lemonade, completed the block of buildings; for the only real and Christian inn in the neighbourhood stood by itself some way down the main road. Between the inn and the hamlet was a crossroads, at which stood a policeman and a uniformed official of a motoring club; and both agreed that Sir Arthur had never passed that point on the road.

It had been at an early hour of a very brilliant summer day that the old gentleman had gone gaily striding up the road, swinging his walking-stick and flapping his yellow gloves. He was a good deal of a dandy, but one of a vigorous and virile sort, especially for his age. His bodily strength and activity were still very remarkable, and his curly hair might have been a yellow so pale as to look white instead of a white that was a faded yellow. His clean-shaven face was handsome, with a high-bridged nose like the Duke of Wellington's; but the most outstanding features were his eyes. They were not merely metaphorically outstanding; something prominent and almost bulging about them was perhaps the only disproportion in his features; but his lips were sensitive and set a little tightly, as if by an act of will. He was the squire of all that country and the owner of the little hamlet. In that sort of place everybody not only knows everybody else, but generally knows where anybody is at any given moment. The normal course would have been for Sir Arthur to walk to the village, to say whatever he wanted to say to the butcher or anybody else, and then walk back to his house again, all in the course of about half an hour: as the two young men did when they had bought their cigarettes. But they saw nobody on the road returning; indeed, there was nobody in sight except the one other guest at the house, a certain Dr Abbott, who was sitting with his broad back to them on the river bank, very patiently fishing.

When all the three guests returned to breakfast, they seemed to think little or nothing of the continued absence of the squire; but when the day wore on and he missed one meal after another, they naturally began to be puzzled, and Sybil Rye, the lady of the household, began to be seriously alarmed. Expeditions of discovery were dispatched to the village again and again without finding any trace; and eventually, when darkness fell, the house was full of a definite fear. Sybil had sent for Father Brown, who was a friend of hers and had helped her out of a difficulty in the past; and under the pressure of the apparent peril he had consented to remain at the house and see it through.

Thus it happened that when the new day's dawn broke without news, Father Brown was early afoot and on the look-out for anything; his black, stumpy figure could be seen pacing the garden path where the garden was embanked along the river, as he scanned the landscape up and down with his short-sighted and rather misty gaze.

He realized that another figure was moving even more

restlessly along the embankment, and saluted Evan Smith, the secretary, by name.

Evan Smith was a tall, fair-haired young man, looking rather harassed, as was perhaps natural in that hour of distraction. But something of the sort hung about him at all times. Perhaps it was more marked because he had the sort of athletic reach and poise and the sort of leonine yellow hair and moustache which accompany (always in fiction and sometimes in fact) a frank and cheerful demeanour of 'English youth'. As in his case they accompanied deep and cavernous eyes and a rather haggard look, the contrast with the conventional tall figure and fair hair of romance may have had a touch of something sinister. But Father Brown smiled at him amiably enough and then said more seriously:

'This is a trying business.'

'It's a very trying business for Miss Rye,' answered the young man gloomily; 'and I don't see why I should disguise what's the worst part of it for me, even if she is engaged to Dalmon. Shocked, I suppose?'

Father Brown did not look very much shocked, but his face was often rather expressionless; he merely said, mildly:

'Naturally, we all sympathize with her anxiety. I suppose you haven't any news or views in the matter?'

'I haven't any news exactly,' answered Smith; 'no news from outside at least. As for views . . .' And he relapsed into moody silence.

'I should be very glad to hear your views,' said the little priest pleasantly. 'I hope you don't mind my saying that you seem to have something on your mind.'

The young man stirred rather than started and looked at the priest steadily, with a frown that threw his hollow eyes into dense shadow.

'Well, you're right enough,' he said at last. 'I suppose I shall have to tell somebody. And you seem a safe sort of person to tell.'

'Do you know what has happened to Sir Arthur?' asked Father Brown calmly, as if it were the most casual matter in the world.

'Yes,' said the secretary harshly, 'I think I know what has happened to Sir Arthur.'

'A beautiful morning,' said a bland voice in his ear; 'a beautiful morning for a rather melancholy meeting.'

This time the secretary jumped as if he had been shot, as the large shadow of Dr Abbott fell across his path in the already strong sunshine. Dr Abbott was still in his dressing-gown – a sumptuous oriental dressing-gown covered with coloured flowers and dragons, looking rather like one of the most brilliant flower-beds that were growing under the glowing sun. He also wore large, flat slippers, which was doubtless why he had come so close to the others without being heard. He would normally have seemed the last person for such a light and airy approach, for he was a very big, broad and heavy man, with a powerful benevolent face very much sunburnt, in a frame of old-fashioned grey whiskers and chin beard, which hung about him luxuriantly, like the long, grey curls of his venerable head. His long slits of eyes were rather sleepy and, indeed, he was an elderly gentleman to be up so early; but he had a look at once robust and weatherbeaten, as of an old farmer or sea captain who had once been out in all weathers. He was the only old comrade and contemporary of the squire in the company that met at the house.

'It seems truly extraordinary,' he said, shaking his head. 'Those little houses are like doll's houses, always open front and back, and there's hardly room to hide anybody, even if they wanted to hide him. And I'm sure they don't. Dalmon and I cross-examined them all yesterday; they're mostly little old women that couldn't hurt a fly. The men are nearly all away harvesting, except the butcher; and Arthur was seen coming out of the butcher's. And nothing could have happened along that stretch by the river, for I was fishing there all day.'

Then he looked at Smith and the look in his long eyes seemed for the moment not only sleepy, but a little sly.

'I think you and Dalmon can testify,' he said, 'that you saw me sitting there through your whole journey there and back.'

'Yes,' said Evan Smith shortly, and seemed rather impatient at the long interruption.

'The only thing I can think of,' went on Dr Abbott slowly; and then the interruption was itself interrupted. A figure at once light and sturdy strode very rapidly across the green lawn between the gay flower-beds, and John Dalmon appeared among them, holding a paper in his hand. He was neatly dressed and rather swarthy, with a very fine square Napoleonic face and very sad eyes – eyes so sad that they looked almost dead. He seemed to be still young, but his black hair had gone prematurely grey about the temples.

'I've just had this telegram from the police,' he said. 'I wired to them last night and they say they're sending down a man at once. Do you know, Dr Abbott, of anybody else we ought to send for? Relations, I mean, and that sort of thing.'

'There is his nephew, Vernon Vaudrey, of course,' said the old man. 'If you will come with me, I think I can give you his address and – and tell you something rather special about him.'

Dr Abbott and Dalmon moved away in the direction of the house and, when they had gone a certain distance, Father Brown said simply, as if there had been no interruption:

'You were saying?'

'You're a cool hand,' said the secretary. 'I suppose it comes of hearing confessions. I feel rather as if I were going to make a confession. Some people would feel a bit jolted out of the mood of confidence by that queer old elephant creeping up like a snake. But I suppose I'd better stick to it, though it really isn't my confession, but somebody else's.' He stopped a moment, frowning and pulling his moustache; then he said, abruptly:

'I believe Sir Arthur has bolted, and I believe I know why.'

There was a silence and then he exploded again.

'I'm in a damnable position, and most people would say I was doing a damnable thing. I am now going to appear in the character of a sneak and a skunk and I believe I am doing my duty.'

'You must be the judge,' said Father Brown gravely. 'What is the matter with your duty?'

'I'm in the perfectly foul position of telling tales against a rival, and a successful rival, too,' said the young man bitterly; 'and I don't know what else in the world I can do. You were asking what was the explanation of Vaudrey's disappearance. I am absolutely convinced that Dalmon is the explanation.'

'You mean,' said the priest, with composure, 'that Dalmon has killed Sir Arthur?'

'No!' exploded Smith, with startling violence. 'No, a hundred times! He hasn't done that, whatever else he's done. He isn't a murderer, whatever else he is. He has the best of all alibis; the evidence of a man who hates him. I'm not likely to perjure myself for love of Dalmon; and I could swear in any court he did nothing to the old man yesterday. Dalmon and I were together all day, or all that part of the day, and he did nothing in the village except buy cigarettes, and nothing here except smoke them and read in the library. No; I believe he is a criminal, but he did not kill Vaudrey. I might even say more; *because* he is a criminal he did not kill Vaudrey.'

'Yes,' said the other patiently, 'and what does that mean?'

'It means,' replied the secretary, 'that he is a criminal committing another crime: and his crime depends on keeping Vaudrey alive.'

'Oh, I see,' said Father Brown.

'I know Sybil Rye pretty well, and her character is a great part of this story. It is a very fine character in both senses: that is, it is of a noble quality and only too delicate a texture. She is one of those people who are terribly conscientious, without any of that armour of habit and hard common sense that many conscientious people get. She is almost insanely sensitive and at the same time quite unselfish. Her history is curious: she was left literally penniless like a foundling and Sir Arthur took her into his house and treated her with consideration, which puzzled many; for, without being hard on the old man, it was not much in his line. But, when she was about seventeen, the explanation came to her with a shock; for her guardian asked her to marry him. Now I come to the curious part of the story. Somehow or other, Sybil had heard from somebody (I rather suspect from old Abbott) that Sir Arthur Vaudrey, in his wilder youth, had committed some crime or, at least, done some great wrong to somebody, which had got him into serious trouble. I don't know what it was. But it was a sort of nightmare to the girl at her crude sentimental age, and made him seem like a monster, at least too much so for the close relation of marriage. What she did was incredibly typical of her. With helpless terror and with heroic courage she told him the truth with her own trembling lips. She admitted that her repulsion might be morbid; she confessed it like a secret madness. To her relief and surprise he took it quietly and courteously, and apparently said no more on the subject; and her sense of his generosity was greatly increased by the next stage of the story. There came into her lonely life the influence of an equally lonely man. He was camping-out like a sort of hermit on one of the islands in the river; and I suppose the mystery made him attractive, though I admit he is attractive enough; a gentleman and quite witty, though very melancholy – which, I suppose, increased the romance. It was this man, Dalmon, of course; and to this day I'm not sure how far she really accepted him; but it got as far as his getting permission to see her guardian. I can fancy her awaiting that interview in an agony of terror and wondering how the old beau would take the appearance of a rival. But here, again, she found she had apparently done him an injustice. He received the younger man with hearty hospitality and seemed to be delighted with the prospects of the young couple. He and Dalmon went shooting and fishing together and were the best of friends, when one day she had another shock. Dalmon let slip in conversation some chance phrase that the old man "had not changed much in thirty years", and the truth about the odd intimacy burst upon her. All that introduction and hospitality had been a masquerade; the men had obviously known each other before. That was why the younger man had come down rather covertly to that district. That was why the elder man was lending himself so readily to promote the match. I wonder what you are thinking?'

'I know what you are thinking,' said Father Brown, with a smile, 'and it seems entirely logical. Here we have Vaudrey, with some ugly story in his past – a mysterious stranger come to haunt him, and getting whatever he wants out of him. In plain words, you think Dalmon is a blackmailer.'

'I do,' said the other; 'and a rotten thing to think, too.'

Father Brown reflected for a moment and then said: 'I think I should like to go up to the house now and have a talk to Dr Abbott.'

When he came out of the house again an hour or two afterwards, he may have been talking to Dr Abbott, but he emerged in company with Sybil Rye, a pale girl with reddish hair and a profile delicate and almost tremulous; at the sight of her, one could instantly understand all the secretary's story of her shuddering candour. It recalled Godiva and certain tales of virgin martyrs; only the shy can be so shameless for conscience's sake. Smith came forward to meet them, and for a moment they stood talking on the lawn. The day which had been brilliant from daybreak was now glowing and even glaring; but Father Brown carried his black bundle of an umbrella as well as wearing his black umbrella of a hat; and seemed, in a general way, buttoned up to breast the storm. But perhaps it was only an unconscious effect of attitude; and perhaps the storm was not a material storm.

'What I hate about it all,' Sybil was saying in a low voice, 'is the talk that's beginning already; suspicions against everybody. John and Evan can answer for each other, I suppose; but Dr Abbott has had an awful scene with the butcher, who thinks he is accused and is throwing accusations about in consequence.'

Evan Smith looked very uncomfortable; then blurted out:

'Look here, Sybil, I can't say much, but we don't believe there's any need for all that. It's all very beastly, but we don't think there's been – any violence.'

'Have you got a theory, then?' said the girl, looking instantly at the priest.

'I have heard a theory,' he replied, 'which seems to me very convincing.'

He stood looking rather dreamily towards the river; and Smith and Sybil began to talk to each other swiftly, in lowered tones. The priest drifted along the river bank, ruminating, and plunged into a plantation of thin trees on an almost overhanging bank. The strong sun beat on the thin veil of little dancing leaves like small green flames, and all the birds were singing as if the tree had a hundred tongues. A minute or two later, Evan Smith heard his own name called cautiously and yet clearly from the green depths of the thicket. He stepped rapidly in that direction and met Father Brown returning. The priest said to him, in a very low voice:

'Don't let the lady come down here. Can't you get rid of her? Ask her to telephone or something; and then come back here again.'

Evan Smith turned with a rather desperate appearance of carelessness and approached the girl; but she was not the sort of person whom it is hard to make busy with small jobs for others. In a very short time she had vanished into the house and Smith turned to find that Father Brown had once more vanished into the thicket. Just beyond the clump of trees was a sort of small chasm where the turf had subsided to the level of the sand by the river. Father Brown was standing on the brink of this cleft, looking down; but, either by accident or design, he was holding his hat in his hand, in spite of the strong sun pouring on his head.

'You had better see this yourself,' he said, heavily, 'as a matter of evidence. But I warn you to be prepared.'

'Prepared for what?' asked the other.

'Only for the most horrible thing I ever saw in my life,' said Father Brown.

Evan Smith stepped to the brink of the bank of turf and with difficulty repressed a cry rather like a scream.

Sir Arthur Vaudrey was glaring and grinning up at him; the face was turned up so that he could have put his foot on it; the head was thrown back, with its wig of whitish yellow hair towards him, so that he saw the face upside down. This made it seem all the more like a part of a nightmare; as if a man were walking about with his head stuck on the wrong way. What was he doing? Was it possible that Vaudrey was really creeping about, hiding in the cracks of field and bank, and peering out at them in this unnatural posture? The rest of the figure seemed hunched and almost crooked, as if it had been crippled or deformed, but on looking more closely, this seemed only the foreshortening of limbs fallen in a heap. Was he mad? Was he? The more Smith looked at him the stiffer the posture seemed.

'You can't see it from here properly,' said Father Brown, 'but his throat is cut.'

Smith shuddered suddenly. 'I can well believe it's the most horrible thing you've seen,' he said. 'I think it's seeing the face upside down. I've seen that face at breakfast, or dinner, every day for ten years; and it always looked quite pleasant and polite. You turn it upside down and it looks like the face of a fiend.'

'The face really is smiling,' said Father Brown, soberly; 'which is perhaps not the least part of the riddle. Not many men smile while their throats are being cut, even if they do it themselves. That smile, combined with those gooseberry eyes of his that always seemed standing out of his head, is enough, no doubt, to explain the expression. But it's true, things look different upside down. Artists often turn their drawings upside down to test their correctness. Sometimes, when it's difficult to turn the object itself upside down (as in the case of the Matterhorn, let us say), they have been known to stand on their heads, or at least look between their legs.'

The priest, who was talking thus flippantly to steady the other man's nerves, concluded by saying, in a more serious tone: 'I quite understand how it must have upset you. Unfortunately, it also upset something else.'

'What do you mean?'

'It has upset the whole of our very complete theory,' replied the other; and he began clambering down the bank on to the little strip of sand by the river.

'Perhaps he did it himself,' said Smith abruptly. 'After all, that's the most obvious sort of escape, and fits in with our theory very well. He wanted a quiet place and he came here and cut his throat.'

'He didn't come here at all,' said Father Brown. 'At least, not alive, and not by land. He wasn't killed here; there's not enough blood. This sun has dried his hair and clothes pretty well by now; but there are the traces of two trickles of water in the sand. Just about here the tide comes up from the sea and makes an eddy that washed the body into the creek and left it when the tide retired. But the body must first have been washed down the river, presumably from the village, for the river runs just behind the row of little houses and shops. Poor Vaudrey died up in the hamlet, somehow; after all, I don't think he committed suicide; but the trouble is who would, or could, have killed him up in that potty little place?'

He began to draw rough designs with the point of his stumpy umbrella on the strip of sand.

'Let's see; how does the row of shops run? First, the butcher's; well, of course, a butcher would be an ideal performer with a large carving-knife. But you saw Vaudrey come out, and it isn't very probable that he stood in the outer shop while the butcher said: "Good morning. Allow me to cut your throat! Thank you. And the next article, please?" Sir Arthur doesn't strike me as the sort of man who'd have stood there with a pleasant smile while this happened. He was a very strong and vigorous man, with rather a violent temper. And who else, except the butcher, could have stood up to him? The next shop is kept by an old woman. Then comes the tobacconist, who is certainly a man, but I am told quite a small and timid one. Then there is the dressmaker's, run by two maiden ladies, and then a refreshment shop run by a man who happens to be in hospital and who has left his wife in charge. There are two or three village lads, assistants and errand boys, but they were away on a special job. The refreshment shop ends the street; there is nothing beyond that but the inn, with the policeman between.'

He made a punch with the ferrule of his umbrella to represent the policeman, and remained moodily staring up the river. Then he made a slight movement with his hand and, stepping quickly across, stooped over the corpse.

'Ah,' he said, straightening himself and letting out a great breath. 'The tobacconist! Why in the world didn't I remember that about the tobacconist?'

'What is the matter with you?' demanded Smith in some exasperation; for Father Brown was rolling his eyes and muttering, and he had uttered the word 'tobacconist' as if it were a terrible word of doom.

'Did you notice,' said the priest, after a pause, 'something rather curious about his face?'

'Curious, my God!' said Evan, with a retrospective shudder. 'Anyhow, his throat was cut . . .'

'I said his face,' said the cleric quietly. 'Besides, don't you notice he has hurt his hand and there's a small bandage round it?'

'Oh, that has nothing to do with it,' said Evan hastily. 'That happened before and was quite an accident. He cut his hand with a broken ink-bottle while we were working together.'

'It has something to do with it, for all that,' replied Father Brown.

There was a long silence, and the priest walked moodily along the sand, trailing his umbrella and sometimes muttering the word 'tobacconist', till the very word chilled his friend with fear. Then he suddenly lifted the umbrella and pointed to a boat-house among the rushes.

'Is that the family boat?' he asked. 'I wish you'd just scull me up the river; I want to look at those houses from the back. There's no time to lose. They may find the body; but we must risk that.'

Smith was already pulling the little boat upstream towards the hamlet before Father Brown spoke again. Then he said:

'By the way, I found out from old Abbott what was the real story about poor Vaudrey's misdemeanour. It was a rather curious story about an Egyptian official who had insulted him by saying that a good Moslem would avoid swine and Englishmen, but preferred swine; or some such tactful remark. Whatever happened at the time, the quarrel was apparently renewed some years after, when the official visited England; and Vaudrey, in his violent passion, dragged the man to a pig-sty on the farm attached to the country house and threw him in, breaking his arm and leg and leaving him there till next morning. There was rather a row about it, of course, but many people thought Vaudrey had acted in a pardonable passion of patriotism. Anyhow, it seems not quite the thing that would have kept a man silent under deadly blackmail for decades.'

'Then you don't think it had anything to do with the story we are considering?' asked the secretary, thoughtfully.

'I think it had a thundering lot to do with the story I am considering now,' said Father Brown.

They were now floating past the low wall and the steep strips of back garden running down from the back doors to the river. Father Brown counted them carefully, pointing with his umbrella, and when he came to the third he said again:

'Tobacconist! Is the tobacconist by any chance. . .? But I think I'll act on my guess till I know. Only, I'll tell you what it was I thought odd about Sir Arthur's face.'

'And what was that?' asked his companion, pausing and resting on his oars for an instant.

'He was a great dandy,' said Father Brown, 'and the face was only half-shaved . . . Could you stop here a moment? We could tie up the boat to that post.'

A minute or two afterwards they had clambered over the little wall and were mounting the steep cobbled paths of the little garden, with its rectangular beds of vegetables and flowers.

'You see, the tobacconist *does* grow potatoes,' said Father Brown. 'Associations with Sir Walter Raleigh, no doubt. Plenty of potatoes and plenty of potato sacks. These little country people have not lost all the habits of peasants; they still run two or three jobs at once. But country tobacconists very often do one odd job extra, that I never thought of till I saw Vaudrey's chin. Nine times out of ten you *call* the shop the tobacconist's, but it *is* also the barber's. He'd cut his hand and couldn't shave himself; so he came up here. Does that suggest anything else to you?'

'It suggests a good deal,' replied Smith; 'but I expect it will suggest a good deal more to you.'

'Does it suggest, for instance,' observed Father Brown, 'the only conditions in which a vigorous and rather violent gentleman might be smiling pleasantly when his throat was cut?'

The next moment they had passed through a dark passage or two at the back of the house, and came into the back room of the shop, dimly lit by filtered light from beyond and a dingy and cracked looking-glass. It seemed, somehow, like the green twilight of a tank; but there was light enough to see the rough apparatus of a barber's shop and the pale and even panic-stricken face of a barber.

Father Brown's eye roamed round the room, which seemed to have been just recently cleaned and tidied, till his gaze found something in a dusty corner just behind the door. It was a hat hanging on a hat-peg. It was a white hat, and one very well known to all that village. And yet, conspicuous as it had always seemed in the street, it seemed only an example of the sort of little thing a certain sort of man often entirely forgets, when he has most carefully washed floors or destroyed stained rags.

'Sir Arthur Vaudrey was shaved here yesterday morning, I think,' said Father Brown in a level voice.

To the barber, a small, bald-headed, spectacled man whose name was Wicks, the sudden appearance of these two figures out of his own back premises was like the appearance of two ghosts risen out of a grave under the floor. But it was at once apparent that he had more to frighten him than any fancy of superstition. He shrank, we might almost say that he shrivelled, into a corner of the dark room; and everything about him seemed to dwindle, except his great goblin spectacles.

'Tell me one thing,' continued the priest, quietly. 'You had a reason for hating the squire?'

The man in the corner babbled something that Smith could not hear; but the priest nodded.

'I know you had,' he said. 'You hated him; and that's how I know you didn't kill him. Will you tell us what happened, or shall I?'

There was a silence filled with the faint ticking of a clock in the back kitchen; and then Father Brown went on.

'What happened was this. When Mr Dalmon stepped inside your outer shop, he asked for some cigarettes that were in the window. You stepped outside for a moment, as shopmen often do, to make sure of what he meant; and in that moment of time he perceived in the inner room the razor you had just laid down, and the yellow-white head of Sir Arthur in the barber's chair; probably both glimmering in the light of that little window beyond. It took but an instant for him to pick up the razor and cut the throat and come back to the counter. The victim would not even be alarmed at the razor and the hand. He died smiling at his own thoughts. And what thoughts! Nor, I think, was Dalmon alarmed. He had done it so quickly and quietly that Mr Smith here could have sworn in court that the two were together all the time. But there was somebody who was alarmed, very legitimately, and that was you. You had quarrelled with your landlord about arrears of rent and so on; you came back into your own shop and found your enemy murdered in your own chair, with your own razor. It was not altogether unnatural that you despaired of clearing yourself, and preferred to clear up the mess; to clean the floor and throw the corpse into the river at night, in a potato sack rather loosely tied. It was rather lucky that there were fixed hours after which your barber's shop was shut; so you had plenty of time. You seem to have remembered everything but the hat . . . Oh, don't be frightened; I shall forget everything, including the hat.'

And he passed placidly through the outer shop into the street beyond, followed by the wondering Smith, and leaving behind the barber, stunned and staring.

'You see,' said Father Brown to his companion, 'it was one of those cases where a motive really is too weak to convict a man and yet strong enough to acquit him. A little nervous fellow like that would be the last man *really* to kill a big strong man for a tiff about money. But he would be the first man to fear that he would be accused of having done it . . . Ah, there was a thundering difference in the motive of the man who did do it.' And he relapsed into reflection, staring and almost glaring at vacancy.

'It is simply awful,' groaned Evan Smith. 'I was abusing Dalmon as a blackmailer and a blackguard an hour or two ago, and yet it breaks me all up to hear he really did this, after all.'

The priest still seemed to be in a sort of trance, like a man staring down into an abyss. At last his lips moved and he murmured, more as if it were a prayer than an oath: 'Merciful God, what a horrible revenge!'

His friend questioned him, but he continued as if talking to himself.

'What a horrible tale of hatred! What a vengeance for one mortal worm to take on another! Shall we ever get to the bottom of this bottomless human heart, where such abominable imaginations can abide? God save us all from pride; but I cannot yet make any picture in my mind of hate and vengeance like that.'

'Yes,' said Smith; 'and I can't quite picture why he should kill Vaudrey at all. If Dalmon was a blackmailer, it would seem more natural for Vaudrey to kill him. As you say, the throat-cutting was a horrid business, but –'

Father Brown started, and blinked like a man awakened from sleep.

'Oh, *that!*' he corrected hastily. 'I wasn't thinking about that. I didn't mean the murder in the barber's shop, when – when I said a horrible tale of vengeance. I was thinking of a much more horrible tale than that; though, of course, that was horrible enough, in its way. But that was much more comprehensible; almost anybody might have done it. In fact, it was very nearly an act of self-defence.'

'*What?*' exclaimed the secretary incredulously. 'A man creeps up behind another man and cuts his throat, while he is smiling pleasantly at the ceiling in a barber's chair, and you say it was self-defence!'

'I do not say it was justifiable self-defence,' replied the other. 'I only say that many a man would have been driven to it, to defend himself against an appalling calamity – which was also an appalling crime. It was that other crime that I was thinking about. To begin with, about that question you asked just now – why should the blackmailer be the murderer? Well, there are a good many conventional confusions and errors on a point like that.' He paused, as if collecting his thoughts after his recent trance of horror, and went on in ordinary tones.

'You observe that two men, an older and a younger, go about together and agree on a matrimonial project; but the origin of their intimacy is old and concealed. One is rich and the other poor; and you guess at blackmail. You are quite right, at least to that extent. Where you are quite wrong is in guessing which is which. You assume that the poor man was blackmailing the rich man. As a matter of fact, the rich man was blackmailing the poor man.'

'But that seems nonsense,' objected the secretary.

'It is much worse than nonsense; but it is not at all uncommon,' replied the other. 'Half modern politics consists of rich men blackmailing people. Your notion that it's nonsense rests on two illusions which are both nonsensical. One is, that rich men never want to be richer; the other is, that a man can only be blackmailed for money. It's the last that is in question here. Sir Arthur Vaudrey was acting not for avarice, but for vengeance. And he planned the most hideous vengeance I ever heard of.'

'But why should he plan vengeance on John Dalmon?' inquired Smith.

'It wasn't on John Dalmon that he planned vengeance,' replied the priest, gravely.

There was a silence; and he resumed, almost as if changing the subject. 'When we found the body, you remember, we saw the face upside down; and you said it looked like the face of a fiend. Has it occurred to you that the murderer also saw the face upside down, coming behind the barber's chair?'

'But that's all morbid extravagance,' remonstrated his companion. 'I was quite used to the face when it was the right way up.'

'Perhaps you have never seen it the right way up,' said Father Brown. 'I told you that artists turn a picture the wrong way up when they want to see it the right way up. Perhaps, over all those breakfasts and tea-tables, you had got used to the face of a fiend.'

'What on earth are you driving at?' demanded Smith, impatiently.

'I speak in parables,' replied the other in a rather sombre tone. 'Of course, Sir Arthur was not actually a fiend; he was a man with a character which he had made out of a temperament that might also have been turned to good. But those goggling, suspicious eyes; that tight, yet quivering mouth, might have told you something if you had not been so used to them. You know, there are physical bodies on which a wound will not heal. Sir Arthur had a mind of that sort. It was as if it lacked a skin; he had a feverish vigilance of vanity; those strained eyes were open with an insomnia of egoism. Sensibility need not be selfishness. Sybil Rye, for instance, has the same thin skin and manages to be a sort of saint. But Vaudrey had turned it all to poisonous pride; a pride that was not even secure and self-satisfied. Every scratch on the surface of his soul festered. And *that* is the meaning of that old story about throwing the man into the pig-sty. If he'd thrown him then and there, after being called a pig, it might have been a pardonable burst of passion. But there was no pig-sty; and that is just the point. Vaudrey remembered the silly insult for years and years, till he could get the Oriental into the improbable neighbourhood of a pig-sty; and then he took what he considered the only appropriate and artistic revenge . . . Oh, my God! he liked his revenges to be appropriate and artistic.'

Smith looked at him curiously. 'You are not thinking of the pig-sty story,' he said.

'No,' said Father Brown; 'of the other story.' He controlled the shudder in his voice, and went on:

'Remembering that story of a fantastic and yet patient plot to make the vengeance fit the crime, consider the other story before us. Had anybody else, to your knowledge, ever insulted Vaudrey, or offered him what he thought a mortal insult? Yes; a woman insulted him.'

A sort of vague horror began to dawn in Evan's eyes; he was listening intently.

'A girl, little more than a child, refused to marry him, because he had once been a sort of criminal; had, indeed, been in prison for a short time for the outrage on the Egyptian. And that madman said, in the hell of his heart: "She shall marry a murderer".'

They took the road towards the great house and went along by the river for some time in silence, before he resumed:

'Vaudrey was in a position to blackmail Dalmon, who had committed a murder long ago; probably he knew of several crimes among the wild comrades of his youth. Probably it was a wild crime with some redeeming features; for the wildest murders are never the worst. And Dalmon looks to me like a man who knows remorse, even for killing Vaudrey. But he was in Vaudrey's power and, between them, they entrapped the girl very cleverly into an engagement; letting the lover try his luck first, for instance, and the other only encouraging magnificently. But Dalmon himself did not know, nobody but the Devil himself did know, what was really in that old man's mind.

'Then, a few days ago, Dalmon made a dreadful discovery. He had obeyed, not altogether unwillingly; he had been a tool; and he suddenly found how the tool was to be broken and thrown away. He came upon certain notes of Vaudrey's in the library which, disguised as they were, told of preparations for giving information to the police. He understood the whole plot and stood stunned as I did when I first understood it. The moment the bride and bridegroom were married, the bridegroom would be arrested and hanged. The fastidious lady, who objected to a husband who had been in prison, should have no husband except a husband on the gallows. That is what Sir Arthur Vaudrey considered an artistic rounding off of the story.'

Evan Smith, deadly pale, was silent; and, far away, down the perspective of the road, they saw the large figure and wide hat of Dr Abbott advancing towards them; even in the outline there was a certain agitation. But they were still shaken with their own private apocalypse.

'As you say, hate is a hateful thing,' said Evan at last; 'and, do you know, one thing gives me a sort of relief. All my hatred of poor Dalmon is gone out of me – now I know how he was twice a murderer.'

It was in silence that they covered the rest of the distance and met the big doctor coming towards them, with his large gloved hands thrown out in a sort of despairing gesture and his grey beard tossing in the wind.

'There is dreadful news,' he said. 'Arthur's body has been found. He seems to have died in his garden.'

'Dear me,' said Father Brown, rather mechanically. 'How dreadful!'

'And there is more,' cried the doctor breathlessly. 'John Dalmon went off to see Vernon Vaudrey, the nephew; but Vernon Vaudrey hasn't heard of him and Dalmon seems to have disappeared entirely.'

'Dear me,' said Father Brown. 'How strange!'

THE WORST CRIME IN THE WORLD

Father Brown was wandering through a picture gallery with an expression that suggested that he had not come there to look at the pictures. Indeed, he did not want to look at the pictures, though he liked pictures well enough. Not that there was anything immoral or improper about those highly modern pictorial designs. He would indeed be of an inflammable temperament who was stirred to any of the more pagan passions by the display of interrupted spirals, inverted cones and broken cylinders with which the art of the future inspired or menaced mankind. The truth is that Father Brown was looking for a young friend who had appointed that somewhat incongruous meeting-place, being herself of a more futuristic turn. The young friend was also a young relative; one of the few relatives that he had. Her name was Elizabeth Fane, simplified into Betty, and she was the child of a sister who had married into a race of refined but impoverished squires. As the squire was dead as well as impoverished, Father Brown stood in the relation of a protector as well as a priest, and in some sense a guardian as well as an uncle. At the moment, however, he was blinking about at the groups in the gallery without catching sight of the familiar brown hair and bright face of his niece. Nevertheless, he saw some people he knew and a number of people he did not know, including some that, as a mere matter of taste, he did not much want to know.

Among the people the priest did not know and who yet aroused his interest was a lithe and alert young man, very beautifully dressed and looking rather like a foreigner, because, while his beard was cut in a spade shape like an old Spaniard's, his dark hair was cropped so close as to look like a tight black skull-cap. Among the people the priest did not particularly want to know was a very dominant-looking lady, sensationally clad in scarlet, with a mane of yellow hair too long to be called bobbed, but too loose to be called anything else. She had a powerful and rather heavy face of a pale and rather unwholesome complexion, and when she looked at anybody she cultivated the fascinations of a basilisk. She towed in attendance behind her a short man with a big beard and a very broad face, with long sleepy slits of eyes. The expression of his face was beaming and benevolent, if only partially awake; but his bull neck, when seen from behind, looked a little brutal.

Father Brown gazed at the lady, feeling that the appearance and approach of his niece would be an agreeable contrast. Yet he continued to gaze, for some reason, until he reached the point of feeling that the appearance of anybody would be an agreeable contrast. It was therefore with a certain relief, though with a slight start as of awakening, that he turned at the sound of his name and saw another face that he knew.

It was the sharp but not unfriendly face of a lawyer named Granby, whose patches of grey hair might almost have been the powder from a wig, so incongruous were they with his youthful energy of movement. He was one of those men in the City who run about like schoolboys in and out of their offices. He could not run round the fashionable picture gallery quite in that fashion; but he looked as if he wanted to, and fretted as he glanced to left and right, seeking somebody he knew.

'I didn't know,' said Father Brown, smiling, 'that you were a patron of the New Art.'

'I didn't know that you were,' retorted the other. 'I came here to catch a man.'

'I hope you will have good sport,' answered the priest. 'I'm doing much the same.'

'Said he was passing through to the Continent,' snorted the solicitor, 'and could I meet him in this cranky place.' He ruminated a moment, and said abruptly: 'Look here, I know you can keep a secret. Do you know Sir John Musgrave?'

'No,' answered the priest; 'but I should hardly have thought he was a secret, though they say he does hide himself in a castle. Isn't he the old man they tell all those tales about – how he lives in a tower with a real portcullis and drawbridge, and generally refuses to emerge from the Dark Ages? Is he one of your clients?'

'No,' replied Granby shortly: 'it's his son, Captain Musgrave, who has come to us. But the old man counts for a good deal in the affair, and I don't know him; that's the point. Look here, this is confidential, as I say, but I can confide in you.' He dropped his voice and drew his friend apart into a side gallery containing representations of various real objects, which was comparatively empty.

'This young Musgrave,' he said, 'wants to raise a big sum from us on a *post obit** on his old father in Northumberland. The old man's long past seventy and presumably will *obit* some time or other; but what about the *post*, so to speak? What will happen afterwards to his cash and castles and portcullises and all the rest? It's a very fine old estate, and still worth a lot, but strangely enough it isn't entailed. So you see how we stand. The question is, as the man said in Dickens, is the old man friendly?'

'If he's friendly to his son you'll feel all the friendlier,' observed Father Brown. 'No, I'm afraid I can't help you. I never met Sir John Musgrave, and I understand very few people do meet him nowadays. But it seems obvious you have a right to an answer on that point before you lend the young gentleman your firm's money. Is he the sort that people cut off with a shilling?'

'Well, I'm doubtful,' answered the other. 'He's very popular and brilliant and a great figure in society; but he's a great deal abroad, and he's been a journalist.'

'Well,' said Father Brown, 'that's not a crime. At least not always.'

'Nonsense!' said Granby curtly. 'You know what I mean – he's rather a rolling stone, who's been a journalist and a lecturer and an actor, and all sorts of things. I've got to know where I stand . . . Why, there he is.'

And the solicitor, who had been stamping impatiently about the emptier gallery, turned suddenly and darted into the more crowded room at a run. He was running

* A bond payable after a person's death.

towards the tall and well-dressed young man with the short hair and the foreign-looking beard.

The two walked away together talking, and for some moments afterwards Father Brown followed them with his screwed, short-sighted eyes. His gaze was shifted and recalled, however, by the breathless and even boisterous arrival of his niece, Betty. Rather to the surprise of her uncle, she led him back into the emptier room and planted him on a seat that was like an island in that sea of floor.

'I've got something I must tell you,' she said. 'It's so silly that nobody else will understand it.'

'You overwhelm me,' said Father Brown. 'Is it about this business your mother started telling me about? Engagements and all that; not what the military historians call a general engagement.'

'You know,' she said, 'that she wants me to be engaged to Captain Musgrave.'

'I didn't,' said Father Brown with resignation; 'but Captain Musgrave seems to be quite a fashionable topic.'

'Of course we're very poor,' she said, 'and it's no good saying it makes no difference.'

'Do you want to marry him?' asked Father Brown, looking at her through his half-closed eyes.

She frowned at the floor, and answered in a lower tone:

'I thought I did. At least I think I thought I did. But I've just had rather a shock.'

'Then tell us all about it.'

'I heard him laugh,' she said.

'It is an excellent social accomplishment,' he replied.

'You don't understand,' said the girl. 'It wasn't social

at all. That was just the point of it – that it wasn't social.'

She paused a moment, and then went on firmly:

'I came here quite early, and saw him sitting quite alone in the middle of that gallery with the new pictures, that was quite empty then. He had no idea I or anybody was near; he was sitting quite alone, and he laughed.'

'Well, no wonder,' said Father Brown. 'I'm not an art critic myself, but as a general view of the pictures taken as a whole –'

'Oh, you *won't* understand,' she said almost angrily. 'It wasn't a bit like that. He wasn't looking at the pictures. He was staring right up at the ceiling; but his eyes seemed to be turned inwards, and he laughed so that my blood ran cold.'

The priest had risen and was pacing the room with his hands behind him. 'You mustn't be hasty in a case of this sort,' he began. 'There are two kinds of men – but we can hardly discuss him just now, for here he is.'

Captain Musgrave entered the room swiftly and swept it with a smile. Granby, the lawyer, was just behind him, and his legal face bore a new expression of relief and satisfaction.

'I must apologize for everything I said about the Captain,' he said to the priest as they drifted together towards the door. 'He's a thoroughly sensible fellow and quite sees my point. He asked me himself why I didn't go north and see his old father; I could hear from the old man's own lips how it stood about the inheritance. Well, he couldn't say fairer than that, could he? But he's so anxious to get the thing settled that he offered to take me up in his own car to Musgrave Moss. That's the name of the estate. I suggested that, if he was so kind, we might go together; and we're starting tomorrow morning.'

As they spoke Betty and the Captain came through the doorway together, making in that framework at least a sort of picture that some would be sentimental enough to prefer to cones and cylinders. Whatever their other affinities, they were both very good-looking; and the lawyer was moved to a remark on the fact, when the picture abruptly altered.

Captain James Musgrave looked out into the main gallery, and his laughing and triumphant eyes were riveted on something that seemed to change him from head to foot. Father Brown looked round as under an advancing shadow of premonition; and he saw the lowering, almost livid face of the large woman in scarlet under its leonine yellow hair. She always stood with a slight stoop, like a bull lowering its horns, and the expression of her pale pasty face was so oppressive and hypnotic that they hardly saw the little man with the large beard standing beside her.

Musgrave advanced into the centre of the room towards her, almost like a beautifully dressed waxwork wound up to walk. He said a few words to her that could not be heard. She did not answer; but they turned away together, walking down the long gallery as if in debate, the short, bull-necked man with the beard bringing up the rear like some grotesque goblin page.

'Heaven help us!' muttered Father Brown, frowning after them. 'Who in the world is that woman?'

'No pal of mine, I'm happy to say,' replied Granby with grim flippancy. 'Looks as if a little flirtation with her might end fatally, doesn't it?'

'I don't think he's flirting with her,' said Father Brown.

Even as he spoke the group in question turned at the end of the gallery and broke up, and Captain Musgrave came back to them in hasty strides.

'Look here,' he cried, speaking naturally enough, though they fancied his colour was changed. 'I'm awfully sorry, Mr Granby, but I find I can't come north with you tomorrow. Of course, you will take the car all the same. Please do; I shan't want it. I – I have to be in London for some days. Take a friend with you if you like.'

'My friend, Father Brown –' began the lawyer.

'If Captain Musgrave is really so kind,' said Father Brown gravely. 'I may explain that I have some status in Mr Granby's inquiry, and it would be a great relief to my mind if I could go.'

Which was how it came about that a very elegant car, with an equally elegant chauffeur, shot north the next day over the Yorkshire moors, bearing the incongruous burden of a priest who looked rather like a black bundle, and a lawyer who had the habit of running about on his feet instead of racing on somebody else's wheels.

They broke their journey very agreeably in one of the great dales of the West Riding, dining and sleeping at a comfortable inn, and starting early next day, began to run along the Northumbrian coast till they reached a country that was a maze of sand dunes and rank sea meadows, somewhere in the heart of which lay the old Border castle which had remained so unique and yet so secretive a monument of the old Border wars. They found it at last, by following a path running beside a long arm of the sea that ran inland, and turned eventually into a sort of rude canal ending in the moat of the castle. The castle really was a castle, of the square, embattled plan that the Normans built everywhere from Galilee to the Grampians. It did really and truly have a port-cullis and a drawbridge, and they were very realistically reminded of the fact by an accident that delayed their entrance.

They waded amid long coarse grass and thistle to the bank of the moat which ran in a ribbon of black with dead leaves and scum upon it, like ebony inlaid with a pattern of gold. Barely a yard or two beyond the black ribbon was the other green bank and the big stone pillars of the gateway. But so little, it would seem, had this lonely fastness been approached from outside that when the impatient Granby halloed across to the dim figures behind the portcullis, they seemed to have considerable difficulty even in lowering the great rusty drawbridge. It started on its way, turning over like a great falling tower above them, and then stuck, sticking out in mid-air at a threatening angle.

The impatient Granby, dancing upon the bank, called out to his companion:

'Oh, I can't stand these stick in the mud ways! Why, it'd be less trouble to jump.'

And with characteristic impetuosity he did jump, landing with a slight stagger in safety on the inner shore. Father Brown's short legs were not adapted to jumping. But his temper was more adapted than most people's to falling with a splash into very muddy water. By the promptitude of his companion he escaped falling in very far. But as he was being hauled up the green, slimy bank, he stopped with bent head, peering at a particular point upon the grassy slope.

'Are you botanizing?' asked Granby irritably. 'We've

got no time for you to collect rare plants after your last attempt as a diver among the wonders of the deep. Come on, muddy or no, we've got to present ourselves before the baronet.'

When they had penetrated into the castle, they were received courteously enough by an old servant, the only one in sight, and after indicating their business were shown into a long oak-panelled room with latticed windows of antiquated pattern. Weapons of many different centuries hung in balanced patterns on the dark walls, and a complete suit of fourteenth-century armour stood like a sentinel beside the large fireplace. In another long room beyond could be seen, through the half-open door, the dark colours of the rows of family portraits.

'I feel as if I'd got into a novel instead of a house,' said the lawyer. 'I'd no idea anybody did really keep up the "Mysteries of Udolpho" in this fashion.'

'Yes; the old gentleman certainly carries out his historical craze consistently,' answered the priest; 'and these things are not fakes, either. It's not done by somebody who thinks all medieval people lived at the same time. Sometimes they make up suits of armour out of different bits; but that suit all covered one man, and covered him very completely. You see, it's the late sort of tilting-armour.'

'I think he's a late sort of host, if it comes to that,' grumbled Granby. 'He's keeping us waiting the devil of a time.'

'You must expect everything to go slowly in a place like this,' said Father Brown. 'I think it's very decent of him to see us at all: two total strangers come to ask him highly personal questions.'

And, indeed, when the master of the house appeared they had no reason to complain of their reception; but rather became conscious of something genuine in the traditions of breeding and behaviour that could retain their native dignity without difficulty in that barbarous solitude, and after those long years of rustication and moping. The baronet did not seem either surprised or embarrassed at the rare visitation; though they suspected that he had not had a stranger in his house for a quarter of a lifetime, he behaved as if he had been bowing out duchesses a moment before. He showed neither shyness nor impatience when they touched on the very private matter of their errand; after a little leisurely reflection he seemed to recognize their curiosity as justified under the circumstances. He was a thin, keen-looking old gentleman, with black eyebrows and a long chin, and though the carefully-curled hair he wore was undoubtedly a wig, he had the wisdom to wear the grey wig of an elderly man.

'As regards the question that immediately concerns you,' he said, 'the answer is very simple indeed. I do most certainly propose to hand on the whole of my property to my son, as my father handed it on to me; and nothing – I say advisedly, nothing – would induce me to take any other course.'

'I am most profoundly grateful for the information,' answered the lawyer. 'But your kindness encourages me to say that you are putting it very strongly. I would not suggest that it is in the least likely that your son would do anything to make you doubt his fitness for the charge. Still he might –'

'Exactly,' said Sir John Musgrave dryly, 'he might. It is

rather an understatement to say that he might. Will you be good enough to step into the next room with me for a moment.'

He led them into the further gallery, of which they had already caught a glimpse, and gravely paused before a row of the blackened and lowering portraits.

'This is Sir Roger Musgrave,' he said, pointing to a long-faced person in a black periwig. 'He was one of the lowest liars and rascals in the rascally time of William of Orange, a traitor to two kings and something like the murderer of two wives. That is his father, Sir Robert, a perfectly honest old cavalier. That is his son, Sir James, one of the noblest of the Jacobite martyrs and one of the first men to attempt some reparation to the Church and the poor. Does it matter that the House of Musgrave, the power, the honour, the authority, descended from one good man to another good man through the interval of a bad one? Edward I governed England well. Edward III covered England with glory. And yet the second glory came from the first glory through the infamy and imbecility of Edward II, who fawned upon Gaveston and ran away from Bruce. Believe me, Mr Granby, the greatness of a great house and history is something more than these accidental individuals who carry it on, even though they do not grace it. From father to son our heritage has come down, and from father to son it shall continue. You may assure yourselves, gentlemen, and you may assure my son, that I shall not leave my money to a home for lost cats. Musgrave shall leave it to Musgrave till the heavens fall.'

'Yes,' said Father Brown thoughtfully; 'I see what you mean.'

'And we shall be only too glad,' said the solicitor, 'to convey such a happy assurance to your son.'

'You may convey the assurance,' said their host gravely. 'He is secure in any event of having the castle, the title, the land and the money. There is only a small and merely private addition to that arrangement. Under no circumstances whatever will I ever speak to him as long as I live.'

The lawyer remained in the same respectful attitude, but he was now respectfully staring.

'Why, what on earth has he –'

'I am a private gentleman,' said Musgrave, 'as well as the custodian of a great inheritance. And my son did something so horrible that he has ceased to be – I will not say a gentleman – but even a human being. It is the worst crime in the world. Do you remember what Douglas said when Marmion, his guest, offered to shake hands with him?'

'Yes,' said Father Brown.

'"My castles are my king's alone, from turret to foundation stone,"' said Musgrave. '"The hand of Douglas is his own."'

He turned towards the other room and showed his rather dazed visitors back into it.

'I hope you will take some refreshment,' he said, in the same equable fashion. 'If you have any doubt about your movements, I should be delighted to offer you the hospitality of the castle for the night.'

'Thank you, Sir John,' said the priest in a dull voice, 'but I think we had better go.'

'I will have the bridge lowered at once,' said their host; and in a few moments the creaking of that huge and absurdly antiquated apparatus filled the castle like the grinding of a mill. Rusty as it was, however, it worked successfully this time, and they found themselves standing once more on the grassy bank beyond the moat.

Granby was suddenly shaken by a shudder.

'What in hell was it that his son did?' he cried.

Father Brown made no answer. But when they had driven off again in their car and pursued their journey to a village not far off, called Graystones, where they alighted at the inn of the Seven Stars, the lawyer learned with a little mild surprise that the priest did not propose to travel much farther; in other words, that he had apparently every intention of remaining in the neighbourhood.

'I cannot bring myself to leave it like this,' he said gravely. 'I will send back the car, and you, of course, may very naturally want to go with it. Your question is answered; it is simply whether your firm can afford to lend money on young Musgrave's prospects. But my question isn't answered; it is whether he is a fit husband for Betty. I must try to discover whether he's really done something dreadful, or whether it's the delusion of an old lunatic.'

'But,' objected the lawyer, 'if you want to find out about him, why don't you go after him? Why should you hang about in this desolate hole where he hardly ever comes?'

'What would be the use of my going after him?' asked the other. 'There's no sense in going up to a fashionable young man in Bond Street and saying: "Excuse me, but have you committed a crime too horrible for a human being?" If he's bad enough to do it, he's certainly bad enough to deny it. And we don't even know what it is. No, there's only one man that knows, and *may* tell, in some further outburst of dignified eccentricity. I'm going to keep near him for the present.'

And in truth Father Brown did keep near the eccentric baronet, and did actually meet him on more than one occasion, with the utmost politeness on both sides. For the baronet, in spite of his years, was very vigorous and a great walker, and could often be seen stumping through the village, and along the country lanes. Only the day after their arrival, Father Brown, coming out of the inn on to the cobbled market-place, saw the dark and distinguished figure stride past in the direction of the post office. He was very quietly dressed in black, but his strong face was even more arresting in the strong sunlight; with his silvery hair, swarthy eyebrows and long chin, he had something of a reminiscence of Henry Irving, or some other famous actor. In spite of his hoary hair, his figure as well as his face suggested strength, and he carried his stick more like a cudgel than a crutch. He saluted the priest, and spoke with the same air of coming fearlessly to the point which had marked his revelations of yesterday.

'If you are still interested in my son,' he said, using the terms with an icy indifference, 'you will not see very much of him. He has just left the country. Between ourselves, I might say fled the country.'

'Indeed,' said Father Brown with a grave stare.

'Some people I never heard of, called Grunov, have been pestering me, of all people, about his whereabouts,' said Sir John; 'and I've just come in to send off a wire to tell them that, so far as I know, he's living in the Poste Restante, Riga. Even that has been a nuisance. I came in yesterday to do it, but was five minutes too late for the post office. Are you staying long? I hope you will pay me another visit.'

When the priest recounted to the lawyer his little interview with old Musgrave in the village, the lawyer was both puzzled and interested.

'Why has the Captain bolted?' he asked. 'Who are the other people who want him? Who on earth are the Grunovs?'

'For the first, I don't know,' replied Father Brown. 'Possibly his mysterious sin has come to light. I should rather guess that the other people are blackmailing him about it. For the third, I think I do know. That horrible fat woman with yellow hair is called Madame Grunov, and that little man passes as her husband.'

The next day Father Brown came in rather wearily, and threw down his black bundle of an umbrella with the air of a pilgrim laying down his staff. He had an air of some depression. But it was as it was so often in his criminal investigations. It was not the depression of failure, but the depression of success.

'It's rather a shock,' he said in a dull voice; 'but I ought to have guessed it. I ought to have guessed it when I first went in and saw the thing standing there.'

'When you saw what?' asked Granby impatiently.

'When I saw there was only one suit of armour,' answered Father Brown.

There was a silence during which the lawyer only stared at his friend, and then the friend resumed.

'Only the other day I was just going to tell my niece

that there are two types of men who can laugh when they are alone. One might almost say the man who does it is either very good or very bad. You see, he is either confiding the joke to God or confiding it to the Devil. But anyhow he has an inner life. Well, there really is a kind of man who confides the joke to the Devil. He does not mind if nobody sees the joke; if nobody can safely be allowed even to know the joke. The joke is enough in itself, if it is sufficiently sinister and malignant.'

'But what are you talking about?' demanded Granby. '*Whom* are you talking about? Which of them, I mean? *Who* is this person who is having a sinister joke with his Satanic Majesty?'

Father Brown looked across at him with a ghastly smile.

'Ah,' he said, 'that's the joke.'

There was another silence, but this time the silence seemed to be rather full and oppressive than merely empty; it seemed to settle down on them like the twilight that was gradually turning from dusk to dark. Father Brown went on speaking in a level voice, sitting stolidly with his elbows on the table.

'I've been looking up the Musgrave family,' he said. 'They are vigorous and long-lived stock, and even in the ordinary way I should think you would wait a good time for your money.'

'We're quite prepared for that,' answered the solicitor; 'but anyhow it can't last indefinitely. The old man is nearly eighty, though he still walks about, and the people at the inn here laugh and say they don't believe he will ever die.'

Father Brown jumped up with one of his rare but rapid

movements, but remained with his hands on the table, leaning forward and looking his friend in the face.

'That's it,' he cried in a low but excited voice. 'That's the only problem. That's the only real difficulty. How will he die? How on earth is he to die?'

'What on earth do you mean?' asked Granby.

'I mean,' came the voice of the priest out of the darkening room, 'that I know the crime that James Musgrave committed.'

His tones had such a chill in them that Granby could hardly repress a shiver; he murmured a further question.

'It was really the worst crime in the world,' said Father Brown. 'At least, many communities and civilizations have accounted it so. It was always from the earliest times marked out in tribe and village for tremendous punishment. But anyhow, I know now what young Musgrave really did and why he did it.'

'And what did he do?' asked the lawyer.

'He killed his father,' answered the priest.

The lawyer in his turn rose from his seat and gazed across the table with wrinkled brows.

'But his father is at the castle,' he cried in sharp tones.

'His father is in the moat,' said the priest, 'and I was a fool not to have known it from the first when something bothered me about that suit of armour. Don't you remember the look of that room? How very carefully it was arranged and decorated? There were two crossed battleaxes hung on one side of the fireplace, two crossed battleaxes on the other. There was a round Scottish shield on one wall, a round Scottish shield on the other. And there was a stand of armour guarding one side of the hearth, and an empty space on the other. Nothing will make me believe that a man who arranged all the rest of that room with that exaggerated symmetry left that one feature of it lopsided. There was almost certainly another man in armour. And what has become of him?'

He paused a moment, and then went on in a more matter-of-fact tone:

'When you come to think of it, it's a very good plan for a murder, and meets the permanent problem of the disposal of the body. The body could stand inside that complete tilting-armour for hours; or even days, while servants came and went, until the murderer could simply drag it out in the dead of night and lower it into the moat, without even crossing the bridge. And then what a good chance he ran! As soon as the body was at all decayed in the stagnant water there would sooner or later be nothing but a skeleton in fourteenth-century armour, a thing very likely to be found in the moat of an old Border castle. It was unlikely that anybody would look for anything there, but if they did, that would soon be all they would find. And I got some confirmation of that. That was when you said I was looking for a rare plant; it was a plant in a good many senses, if you'll excuse the jest. I saw the marks of two feet sunk so deep into the solid bank I was sure that the man was either very heavy or was carrying something very heavy. Also, by the way, there's another moral from that little incident when I made my celebrated graceful and cat-like leap.'

'My brain is rather reeling,' said Granby, 'but I begin to have some notion of what all this nightmare is about. What about you and your cat-like leap?'

'At the post office today,' said Father Brown, 'I casually

confirmed the statement the baronet made to me yesterday, that he had been there just after closing-time on the
day previous – that is, not only on the very day we
arrived, but at the very time we arrived. Don't you see
what that means? It means that he was actually out when
we called, and came back while we were waiting; and
that was why we had to wait so long. And when I saw
that, I suddenly saw a picture that told the whole story.'

'Well,' asked the other impatiently, 'and what about
it?'

'An old man of eighty can walk,' said Father Brown.
'An old man can even walk a good deal, pottering about
in country lanes. But an old man can't *jump*. He would be
an even less graceful jumper than I was. Yet, if the
baronet came back while we were waiting, he must have
come in as we came in – by jumping the moat – for the
bridge wasn't lowered till later. I rather guess he had
hampered it himself to delay inconvenient visitors, to
judge by the rapidity with which it was repaired. But that
doesn't matter. When I saw that fancy picture of the black
figure with the grey hair taking a flying leap across the
moat I knew instantly that it was a young man dressed
up as an old man. And there you have the whole
story.'

'You mean,' said Granby slowly, 'that this pleasing
youth killed his father, hid the corpse first in the armour
and then in the moat, disguised himself and so on?'

'They happened to be almost exactly alike,' said the
priest. 'You could see from the family portraits how
strong the likeness ran. And then you talk of his disguis-
ing himself. But in a sense everybody's dress is a disguise. The old man disguised himself in a wig, and the

young man in a foreign beard. When he shaved and put the wig on his cropped head he was exactly like his father, with a little make-up. Of course, you understand now why he was so very polite about getting you to come up next day here by car. It was because he himself was coming up that night by train. He got in front of you, committed his crime, assumed his disguise, and was ready for the legal negotiations.'

'Ah,' said Granby thoughtfully, 'the legal negotiations! You mean, of course, that the real old baronet would have negotiated very differently.'

'He would have told you plainly that the Captain would never get a penny,' said Father Brown. 'The plot, queer as it sounds, was really the only way of preventing his telling you so. But I want you to appreciate the cunning of what the fellow did tell you. His plan answered several purposes at once. He was being blackmailed by these Russians for some villainy; I suspect for treason during the war. He escaped from them at a stroke, and probably sent them chasing off to Riga after him. But the most beautiful refinement of all was that theory he enunciated about recognizing his son as an heir, but not as a human being. Don't you see that while it secured the *post obit*, it also provided some sort of answer to what would soon be the greatest difficulty of all?'

'I see several difficulties,' said Granby; 'which one do you mean?'

'I mean that if the son was not even disinherited, it would look rather odd that the father and son never met. The theory of a private repudiation answered that. So there only remained one difficulty, as I say, which is probably perplexing the gentleman now. How on earth is the old man to die?'

'I know how he ought to die,' said Granby.

Father Brown seemed to be a little bemused, and went on in a more abstracted fashion.

'And yet there is something more in it than that,' he said. 'There was something about that theory that he liked in a way that is more – well, more theoretical. It gave him an insane intellectual pleasure to tell you in one character that he had committed a crime in another character – when he really had. That is what I mean by the infernal irony; by the joke shared with the Devil. Shall I tell you something that sounds like what they call a paradox? Sometimes it is a joy in the very heart of hell to tell the truth. And above all, to tell it so that everybody misunderstands it. That is why he liked that antic of pretending to be somebody else, and then painting himself as black – as he was. And that was why my niece heard him laughing to himself all alone in the picture gallery.'

Granby gave a slight start, like a person brought back to common things with a bump.

'Your niece,' he cried. 'Didn't her mother want her to marry Musgrave? A question of wealth and position, I suppose.'

'Yes,' said Father Brown dryly; 'her mother was all in favour of a prudent marriage.'

THE GREEN MAN

A young man in knickerbockers, with an eager sanguine profile, was playing golf against himself on the links that lay parallel to the sand and sea, which were all growing grey with twilight. He was not carelessly knocking a ball about, but rather practising particular strokes with a sort of microscopic fury; like a neat and tidy whirlwind. He had learned many games quickly, but he had a disposition to learn them a little more quickly than they can be learnt. He was rather prone to be a victim of those remarkable invitations by which a man may learn the Violin in Six Lessons – or acquire a perfect French accent by a Correspondence Course. He lived in the breezy atmosphere of such hopeful advertisement and adventure. He was at present the private secretary of Admiral Sir Michael Craven, who owned the big house behind the park abutting on the links. He was ambitious, and had no intention of continuing indefinitely to be private secretary to anybody. But he was also reasonable; and he knew that the best way of ceasing to be a secretary was to be a good secretary. Consequently he was a very good secretary; dealing with the ever-accumulating arrears of the Admiral's correspondence with the same swift

centripetal concentration with which he addressed the
golf ball. He had to struggle with the correspondence
alone and at his own discretion at present; for the
Admiral had been with his ship for the last six months;
and, though now returning, was not expected for hours,
or possibly days.

With an athletic stride, the young man, whose name
was Harold Harker, crested the rise of turf that was the
rampart of the links and, looking out across the sands to
the sea, saw a strange sight. He did not see it very clearly;
for the dusk was darkening every minute under stormy
clouds; but it seemed to him, by a sort of momentary
illusion, like a dream of days long past or a drama played
by ghosts, out of another age in history.

The last of the sunset lay in long bars of copper and
gold above the last dark strip of sea that seemed rather
black than blue. But blacker still against this gleam in the
west, there passed in sharp outline, like figures in a shadow pantomime, two men with three-cornered cocked
hats and swords; as if they had just landed from one of
the wooden ships of Nelson. It was not at all the sort of
hallucination that would have come natural to Mr Harker, had he been prone to hallucinations. He was of the
type that is at once sanguine and scientific; and would be
more likely to fancy the flying-ships of the future than the
fighting-ships of the past. He therefore very sensibly
came to the conclusion that even a futurist can believe his
eyes.

His illusion did not last more than a moment. On the
second glance, what he saw was unusual but not incredible. The two men who were striding in single file across
the sands, one some fifteen yards behind the other, were

ordinary modern naval officers; but naval officers wearing that almost extravagant full-dress uniform which naval officers never do wear if they can possibly help it; only on great ceremonial occasions such as the visits of Royalty. In the man walking in front, who seemed more or less unconscious of the man walking behind, Harker recognized at once the high-bridged nose and spike-shaped beard of his own employer the Admiral. The other man following in his tracks he did not know. But he did know something about the circumstances connected with the ceremonial occasion. He knew that when the Admiral's ship put in at the adjacent port, it was to be formally visited by a Great Personage; which was enough, in that sense, to explain the officers being in full dress. But he did also know the officers; or at any rate the Admiral. And what could have possessed the Admiral to come on shore in that rig-out, when one could swear he would seize five minutes to change into mufti or at least into undress uniform, was more than his secretary could conceive. It seemed somehow to be the very last thing he would do. It was indeed to remain for many weeks one of the chief mysteries of this mysterious business. As it was, the outline of these fantastic court uniforms against the empty scenery, striped with dark sea and sand, had something suggestive of comic opera; and reminded the spectator of *Pinafore*.

The second figure was much more singular; somewhat singular in appearance, despite his correct lieutenant's uniform, and still more extraordinary in behaviour. He walked in a strangely irregular and uneasy manner; sometimes quickly and sometimes slowly; as if he could not make up his mind whether to overtake the Admiral or not. The Admiral was rather deaf and certainly heard no footsteps behind him on the yielding sand; but the footsteps behind him, if traced in the detective manner, would have given rise to twenty conjectures from a limp to a dance. The man's face was swarthy as well as darkened with shadow and every now and then the eyes in it shifted and shone, as if to accent his agitation. Once he began to run and then abruptly relapsed into a swaggering slowness and carelessness. Then he did something which Mr Harker could never have conceived any normal naval officer in His Britannic Majesty's Service doing, even in a lunatic asylum. He drew his sword.

It was at this bursting-point of the prodigy that the two passing figures disappeared behind a headland on the shore. The staring secretary had just time to notice the swarthy stranger, with a resumption of carelessness, knock off a head of sea-holly with his glittering blade. He seemed then to have abandoned all idea of catching the other man up. But Mr Harold Harker's face became very thoughtful indeed; and he stood there ruminating for some time before he gravely took himself inland, towards the road that ran past the gates of the great house and so by a long curve down to the sea.

It was up this curving road from the coast that the Admiral might be expected to come, considering the direction in which he had been walking, and making the natural assumption that he was bound for his own door. The path along the sands, under the links, turned inland just beyond the headland and solidifying itself into a road, returned towards Craven House. It was down this road, therefore, that the secretary darted, with characteristic impetuosity, to meet his patron returning home. But the patron was apparently not returning home. What was still more peculiar, the secretary was not returning home either; at least until many hours later; a delay quite long enough to arouse alarm and mystification at Craven House.

Behind the pillars and palms of that rather too palatial country house, indeed, there was expectancy gradually changing to uneasiness. Gryce the butler, a big bilious man abnormally silent below as well as above stairs, showed a certain restlessness as he moved about the main front-hall and occasionally looked out of the side windows of the porch, on the white road that swept towards the sea. The Admiral's sister Marion, who kept house for him, had her brother's high nose with a more sniffy expression; she was voluble, rather rambling, not without humour, and capable of sudden emphasis as shrill as a cockatoo. The Admiral's daughter Olive was dark, dreamy, and as a rule abstractedly silent, perhaps melancholy; so that her aunt generally conducted most of the conversation, and that without reluctance. But the girl also had a gift of sudden laughter that was very engaging.

'I can't think why they're not here already,' said the elder lady. 'The postman distinctly told me he'd seen the Admiral coming along the beach; along with that dreadful creature Rook. Why in the world they call him Lieutenant Rook –'

'Perhaps,' suggested the melancholy young lady, with a momentary brightness, 'perhaps they call him Lieutenant because he is a Lieutenant.'

'I can't think why the Admiral keeps him,' snorted her aunt, as if she were talking of a housemaid. She was very proud of her brother and always called him the Admiral; but her notions of a commission in the Senior Service were inexact.

'Well, Roger Rook is sulky and unsociable and all that,' replied Olive, 'but of course that wouldn't prevent him being a capable sailor.'

'Sailor!' cried her aunt with one of her rather startling cockatoo notes, 'he isn't my notion of a sailor. "The Lass that Loved a Sailor", as they used to sing when I was young . . . Just think of it! He's not gay and free and what's-its-name. He doesn't sing chanties or dance a hornpipe.'

'Well,' observed her niece with gravity. 'The Admiral doesn't very often dance a hornpipe.'

'Oh, you know what I mean – he isn't bright or breezy or anything,' replied the old lady. 'Why, that secretary fellow could do better than that.'

Olive's rather tragic face was transfigured by one of her good and rejuvenating waves of laughter.

'I'm sure Mr Harker would dance a hornpipe for you,' she said, 'and say he had learnt it in half an hour from the book of instructions. He's always learning things of that sort.'

She stopped laughing suddenly and looked at her aunt's rather strained face.

'I can't think why Mr Harker doesn't come,' she added.

'I don't care about Mr Harker,' replied the aunt, and rose and looked out of the window.

The evening light had long turned from yellow to grey and was now turning almost to white under the widening moonlight, over the large flat landscape by the coast; unbroken by any features save a clump of sea-twisted trees round a pool and beyond, rather gaunt and dark against the horizon, the shabby fishermen's tavern on the shore that bore the name of the Green Man. And all that road and landscape was empty of any living thing. Nobody had seen the figure in the cocked hat that had been observed, earlier in the evening, walking by the sea; or the other and stranger figure that had been seen trailing after him. Nobody had even seen the secretary who saw them.

It was after midnight when the secretary at last burst in and aroused the household; and his face, white as a ghost, looked all the paler against the background of the stolid face and figure of a big Inspector of Police. Somehow that red, heavy, indifferent face looked, even more than the white and harassed one, like a mask of doom. The news was broken to the two women with such consideration or concealments as were possible. But the news was that the body of Admiral Craven had been eventually fished out of the foul weeds and scum of the pool under the trees; and that he was drowned and dead.

Anybody acquainted with Mr Harold Harker, secretary, will realize that, whatever his agitation, he was by morning in a mood to be tremendously on the spot. He hustled the Inspector, whom he had met the night before on the road down by the Green Man, into another room for private and practical consultation. He questioned the Inspector rather as the Inspector might have questioned a yokel. But Inspector Burns was a stolid character; and was either too stupid or too clever to resent such trifles. It soon began to look as if he were by no means so stupid as he looked; for he disposed of Harker's eager questions in a manner that was slow but methodical and rational.

'Well,' said Harker (his head full of many manuals with titles like *Be a Detective in Ten Days*). 'Well, it's the old triangle, I suppose. Accident, Suicide or Murder.'

'I don't see how it could be accident,' answered the policeman. 'It wasn't even dark yet and the pool's fifty yards from the straight road that he knew like his own doorstep. He'd no more have got into that pond than he'd go and carefully lie down in a puddle in the street. As for suicide, it's rather a responsibility to suggest it, and rather improbable too. The Admiral was a pretty spry and successful man and frightfully rich, nearly a millionaire in fact; though of course that doesn't prove anything. He seemed to be pretty normal and comfortable in his private life too; he's the last man I should suspect of drowning himself.'

'So that we come,' said the secretary, lowering his voice with the thrill, 'I suppose we come to the third possibility.'

'We won't be in too much of a hurry about that,' said the Inspector to the annoyance of Harker, who was in a hurry about everything. 'But naturally there are one or two things one would like to know. One would like to know about his property, for instance. Do you know who's likely to come in for it? You're his private secretary; do you know anything about his will?'

'I'm not so private a secretary as all that,' answered the young man. 'His solicitors are Messrs Willis, Hardman and Dyke, over in Suttford High Street; and I believe the will is in their custody.'

'Well, I'd better get round and see them pretty soon,' said the Inspector.

'Let's get round and see them at once,' said the impatient secretary.

He took a turn or two restlessly up and down the room and them exploded in a fresh place.

'What have you done about the body, Inspector?' he asked.

'Dr Straker is examining it now at the Police Station. His report ought to be ready in an hour or so.'

'It can't be ready too soon,' said Harker. 'It would save time if we could meet him at the lawyer's.' Then he stopped and his impetuous tone changed abruptly to one of some embarrassment.

'Look here,' he said, 'I want . . . we want to consider the young lady, the poor Admiral's daughter, as much as possible just now. She's got a notion that may be all nonsense; but I wouldn't like to disappoint her. There's some friend of hers she wants to consult, staying in the town at present. Man of the name of Brown; priest or parson of some sort; she's given me his address. I don't take much stock in priests or parsons, but –'

The Inspector nodded. 'I don't take any stock in priests or parsons; but I take a lot of stock in Father Brown,' he said. 'I happened to have to do with him in a queer sort of society jewel case. He ought to have been a policeman instead of a parson.'

'Oh, all right,' said the breathless secretary as he vanished from the room. 'Let him come to the lawyer's too.'

Thus it happened that, when they hurried across to the neighbouring town to meet Dr Straker at the solicitor's office, they found Father Brown already seated there, with his hands folded on his heavy umbrella, chatting pleasantly to the only available member of the firm. Dr Straker also had arrived, but apparently only at that moment, as he was carefully placing his gloves in his top-hat and his top-hat on a side-table. And the mild and beaming expression of the priest's moonlike face and spectacles, together with the silent chuckles of the jolly old grizzled lawyer, to whom he was talking, were enough to show that the doctor had not yet opened his mouth to bring the news of death.

'A beautiful morning after all,' Father Brown was saying. 'That storm seems to have passed over us. There were some big black clouds, but I notice that not a drop of rain fell.'

'Not a drop,' agreed the solicitor toying with a pen; he was the third partner, Mr Dyke; 'there's not a cloud in the sky now. It's the sort of day for a holiday.' Then he realized the newcomers and looked up, laying down the pen and rising. 'Ah, Mr Harker, how are you? I hear the Admiral is expected home soon.' Then Harker spoke, and his voice rang hollow in the room.

'I am sorry to say we are the bearers of bad news. Admiral Craven was drowned before reaching home.'

There was a change in the very air of the still office, though not in the attitudes of the motionless figures; both were staring at the speaker as if a joke had been frozen on their lips. Both repeated the word 'drowned' and looked at each other, and then again at their informant. Then there was a small hubbub of questions.

'When did this happen?' asked the priest.

'Where was he found?' asked the lawyer.

'He was found,' said the Inspector, 'in that pool by the coast, not far from the Green Man, and dragged out all covered with green scum and weeds so as to be almost unrecognizable. But Dr Straker here has – What is the matter, Father Brown? Are you ill?'

'The Green Man,' said Father Brown with a shudder. 'I'm so sorry . . . I beg your pardon for being upset.'

'Upset by what?' asked the staring officer.

'By his being covered with green scum, I suppose,' said the priest, with a rather shaky laugh. Then he added rather more firmly, 'I thought it might have been sea-weed.'

By this time everybody was looking at the priest, with a not unnatural suspicion that he was mad; and yet the next crucial surprise was not to come from him. After a dead silence, it was the doctor who spoke.

Dr Straker was a remarkable man, even to look at. He was very tall and angular, formal and professional in his dress; yet retaining a fashion that has hardly been known since Mid-Victorian times. Though comparatively young, he wore his brown beard very long and spreading over his waistcoat; in contrast with it, his features, which were both harsh and handsome, looked singularly pale. His good looks were also diminished by something in his deep eyes that was not squinting, but like the shadow of a squint. Everybody noticed these things about him, because the moment he spoke, he gave forth an indescribable air of authority. But all he said was:

'There is one more thing to be said, if you come to details, about Admiral Craven being drowned.' Then he added reflectively, 'Admiral Craven was not drowned.'

The Inspector turned with quite a new promptitude and shot a question at him.

'I have just examined the body,' said Dr Straker; 'the cause of death was a stab through the heart with some pointed blade like a stiletto. It was after death, and even some little time after, that the body was hidden in the pool.'

Father Brown was regarding Dr Straker with a very lively eye, such as he seldom turned upon anybody; and when the group in the office began to break up, he managed to attach himself to the medical man for a little further conversation, as they went back down the street. There had not been very much else to detain them except the rather formal question of the will. The impatience of the young secretary had been somewhat tried by the professional etiquette of the old lawyer. But the latter was ultimately induced, rather by the tact of the priest than the authority of the policeman, to refrain from making a mystery where there was no mystery at all. Mr Dyke admitted, with a smile, that the Admiral's will was a very normal and ordinary document, leaving everything to his only child Olive; and that there really was no particular reason for concealing the fact.

The doctor and the priest walked slowly down the street that struck out of the town in the direction of Craven House. Harker had plunged on ahead of him with all his native eagerness to get somewhere; but the two behind seemed more interested in their discussion than their direction. It was in rather an enigmatic tone that the tall doctor said to the short cleric beside him:

'Well, Father Brown, what do you think of a thing like this?'

Father Brown looked at him rather intently for an instant and then said: 'Well, I've begun to think of one or two things; but my chief difficulty is that I only knew the Admiral slightly; though I've seen something of his daughter.'

'The Admiral,' said the doctor with a grim immobility of feature, 'was the sort of man of whom it is said that he had not an enemy in the world.'

'I suppose you mean,' answered the priest, 'that there's something else that will not be said.'

'Oh, it's no affair of mine,' said Straker hastily but rather harshly. 'He had his moods, I suppose. He once threatened me with a legal action about an operation; but I think he thought better of it. I can imagine his being rather rough with a subordinate.'

Father Brown's eyes were fixed on the figure of the secretary striding far ahead; and as he gazed he realized the special cause of his hurry. Some fifty yards farther ahead the Admiral's daughter was dawdling along the road towards the Admiral's house. The secretary soon came abreast of her; and for the remainder of the time Father Brown watched the silent drama of two human backs as they diminished into the distance. The secretary was evidently very much excited about something; but if the priest guessed what it was, he kept it to himself. When he came to the corner leading to the doctor's house, he only said briefly: 'I don't know if you have anything more to tell us.'

'Why should I?' answered the doctor very abruptly; and striding off, left it uncertain whether he was asking why he should have anything to tell, or why he should tell it.

Father Brown went stumping on alone, in the track of the two young people; but when he came to the entrance and avenues of the Admiral's park, he was arrested by the action of the girl, who turned suddenly and came straight towards him; her face unusually pale and her eyes bright with some new and as yet nameless emotion.

'Father Brown,' she said in a low voice, 'I must talk to you as soon as possible. You must listen to me, I can't see any other way out.'

'Why certainly,' he replied, as coolly as if a gutter-boy had asked him the time. 'Where shall we go and talk?'

The girl led him at random to one of the rather tumble-down arbours in the grounds; and they sat down behind a screen of large ragged leaves. She began instantly, as if she must relieve her feelings or faint.

'Harold Harker,' she said, 'has been talking to me about things. Terrible things.'

The priest nodded and the girl went on hastily. 'About Roger Rook. Do you know about Roger?'

'I've been told,' he answered, 'that his fellow-seamen call him The Jolly Roger, because he is never jolly; and looks like the pirate's skull and crossbones.'

'He was not always like that,' said Olive in a low voice. 'Something very queer must have happened to him. I knew him well when we were children; we used to play over there on the sands. He was harum-scarum and always talking about being a pirate; I dare say he was the sort they say might take to crime through reading shockers; but there was something poetical in his way of being piratical. He really was a Jolly Roger then. I suppose he was the last boy who kept up the old legend of really running away to sea; and at last his family had to agree to his joining the Navy. Well . . .'

'Yes,' said Father Brown patiently.

'Well,' she admitted, caught in one of her rare moments of mirth, 'I suppose poor Roger found it disappointing. Naval officers so seldom carry knives in their teeth or wave bloody cutlasses and black flags. But that doesn't explain the change in him. He just stiffened; grew dull and dumb, like a dead man walking about. He always avoids me; but that doesn't matter. I supposed some great grief that's no business of mine had broken him up. And now – well, if what Harold says is true, the grief is neither more nor less than going mad; or being possessed of the devil.'

'And what does Harold say?' asked the priest.

'It's so awful I can hardly say it,' she answered. 'He swears he saw Roger creeping behind my father that night; hesitating and then drawing his sword . . . and the doctor says father was stabbed with a steel point . . . I *can't* believe Roger Rook had anything to do with it. His sulks and my father's temper sometimes led to quarrels; but what are quarrels? I can't exactly say I'm standing up for an old friend; because he isn't even friendly. But you can't help feeling sure of some things, even about an old acquaintance. And yet Harold swears that he –'

'Harold seems to swear a great deal,' said Father Brown.

There was a sudden silence; after which she said in a different tone:

'Well, he does swear other things too. Harold Harker proposed to me just now.'

'Am I to congratulate you, or rather him?' inquired her companion.

'I told him he must wait. He isn't good at waiting.' She was caught again in a ripple of her incongruous sense of the comic: 'He said I was his ideal and his ambition and so on. He has lived in the States; but somehow I never remember it when he is talking about dollars; only when he is talking about ideals.'

'And I suppose,' said Father Brown very softly, 'that it is because you have to decide about Harold that you want to know the truth about Roger.'

She stiffened and frowned, and then equally abruptly smiled, saying: 'Oh, you know too much.'

'I know very little, especially in this affair,' said the priest gravely. 'I only know who murdered your father.' She started up and stood staring down at him stricken white. Father Brown made a wry face as he went on: 'I made a fool of myself when I first realized it; when they'd just been asking where he was found, and went on talking about green scum and the Green Man.'

Then he also rose; clutching his clumsy umbrella with a new resolution, he addressed the girl with a new gravity.

'There is something else that I know, which is the key to all these riddles of yours; but I won't tell you yet. I suppose it's bad news; but it's nothing like so bad as the things you have been fancying.' He buttoned up his coat and turned towards the gate. 'I'm going to see this Mr Rook of yours. In a shed by the shore, near where Mr Harker saw him walking. I rather think he lives there.' And he went bustling off in the direction of the beach.

Olive was an imaginative person; perhaps too imaginative to be safely left to brood over such hints as her friend had thrown out; but he was in rather a hurry to find the best relief for her broodings. The mysterious connection between Father Brown's first shock of enlightenment and the chance language about the pool and the inn, hag-rode her fancy in a hundred forms of ugly symbolism. The Green Man became a ghost trailing loathsome weeds and walking the countryside under the moon; the sign of the Green Man became a human figure hanging as from a gibbet; and the tarn itself became a tavern, a dark subaqueous tavern for the dead sailors. And yet he had taken the most rapid method to overthrow all such nightmares, with a burst of blinding daylight which seemed more mysterious than the night.

For before the sun had set, something had come back into her life that turned her whole world topsy-turvy once more; something she had hardly known that she desired until it was abruptly granted; something that was, like a dream, old and familiar, and yet remained incomprehensible and incredible. For Roger Rook had come striding across the sands, and even when he was a dot in the distance, she knew he was transfigured; and as he came nearer and nearer, she saw that his dark face was alive with laughter and exultation. He came straight towards her, as if they had never parted, and seized her shoulders saying: 'Now I can look after you, thank God.'

She hardly knew what she answered; but she heard herself questioning rather wildly why he seemed so changed and so happy.

'Because I am happy,' he answered. 'I have heard the bad news.'

*

All parties concerned, including some who seemed rather unconcerned, found themselves assembled on the garden path leading to Craven House, to hear the formality, now truly formal, of the lawyer's reading of the will; and the probable, and more practical, sequel of the lawyer's advice upon the crisis. Besides the grey-haired solicitor himself, armed with the testamentary document, there was the Inspector armed with more direct authority touching the crime, and Lieutenant Rook in undisguised attendance on the lady; some were rather mystified on seeing the tall figure of the doctor, some smiled a little on seeing the dumpy figure of the priest. Mr Harker, that Flying Mercury, had shot down to the lodge-gates to meet them, led them back on to the lawn, and then dashed ahead of them again to prepare their reception. He said he would be back in a jiffy; and anyone observing his piston-rod of energy could well believe it; but, for the moment, they were left rather stranded on the lawn outside the house.

'Reminds me of somebody making runs at cricket,' said the Lieutenant.

'That young man,' said the lawyer, 'is rather annoyed that the law cannot move quite so quickly as he does. Fortunately Miss Craven understands our professional difficulties and delays. She has kindly assured me that she still has confidence in my slowness.'

'I wish,' said the doctor, suddenly, 'that I had as much confidence in his quickness.'

'Why, what do you mean?' asked Rook, knitting his brows; 'do you mean that Harker is too quick?'

'Too quick and too slow,' said Dr Straker, in his rather

cryptic fashion. 'I know one occasion at least when he was not so very quick. Why was he hanging about half the night by the pond and the Green Man, before the Inspector came down and found the body? Why did he meet the Inspector? Why should he expect to meet the Inspector outside the Green Man?'

'I don't understand you,' said Rook. 'Do you mean that Harker wasn't telling the truth?'

Dr Straker was silent. The grizzled lawyer laughed with grim good humour.

'I have nothing more serious to say against the young man,' he said, 'than that he made a prompt and praise-worthy attempt to teach me my own business.'

'For that matter, he made an attempt to teach me mine,' said the Inspector, who had just joined the group in front. 'But that doesn't matter. If Dr Straker means anything by his hints, they do matter. I must ask you to speak plainly, doctor. It may be my duty to question him at once.'

'Well, here he comes,' said Rook, as the alert figure of the secretary appeared once more in the doorway.

At this point Father Brown, who had remained silent and inconspicuous at the tail of the procession, aston-ished everybody very much; perhaps, especially those who knew him. He not only walked rapidly to the front, but turned facing the whole group with an arresting and almost threatening expression, like a sergeant bringing soldiers to the halt.

'Stop!' he said almost sternly. 'I apologize to every-body; but it's absolutely necessary that I should see Mr Harker first. I've got to tell him something I know; and I don't think anybody else knows; something he's got to hear. It may save a very tragic misunderstanding with somebody later on.'

'What on earth do you mean?' asked old Dyke the lawyer.

'I mean the bad news,' said Father Brown.

'Here, I say,' began the Inspector indignantly; and then suddenly caught the priest's eye and remembered strange things he had seen in other days. 'Well, if it were anyone in the world but you I should say of all the infernal cheek –'

But Father Brown was already out of hearing, and a moment afterwards was plunged in talk with Harker in the porch. They walked to and fro together for a few paces and then disappeared into the dark interior. It was about twelve minutes afterwards that Father Brown came out alone.

To their surprise he showed no disposition to re-enter the house, now that the whole company were at last about to enter it. He threw himself down on the rather rickety seat in the leafy arbour, and as the procession disappeared through the doorway, lit a pipe and proceeded to stare vacantly at the long ragged leaves about his head and to listen to the birds. There was no man who had a more hearty and enduring appetite for doing nothing.

He was apparently in a cloud of smoke and a dream of abstraction, when the front-doors were once more flung open and two or three figures came out helter-skelter, running towards him, the daughter of the house and her young admirer Mr Rook being easily winners in the race. Their faces were alight with astonishment; and the face of

Inspector Burns, who advanced more heavily behind them, like an elephant shaking the garden, was inflamed with some indignation as well.

'What *can* all this mean?' cried Olive, as she came panting to a halt. 'He's gone!'

'Bolted!' said the Lieutenant explosively. 'Harker's just managed to pack a suitcase and bolted! Gone clean out of the back door and over the garden-wall to God knows where. What *did* you say to him?'

'Don't be silly!' said Olive, with a more worried expression. 'Of course you told him you'd found him out, and now he's gone. I never could have believed he was wicked like that!'

'Well!' gasped the Inspector, bursting into their midst. 'What have you done now? What have you let me down like this for?'

'Well,' repeated Father Brown, 'what have I done?'

'You have let a murderer escape,' cried Burns, with a decision that was like a thunderclap in the quiet garden; 'you have *helped* a murderer to escape. Like a fool I let you warn him; and now he is miles away.'

'I have helped a few murderers in my time, it is true,' said Father Brown; then he added, in careful distinction, 'not, you will understand, helped them to commit the murder.'

'But you knew all the time,' insisted Olive. 'You guessed from the first that it must be he. That's what you meant about being upset by the business of finding the body. That's what the doctor meant by saying my father might be disliked by a subordinate.'

'That's what I complain of,' said the official indignantly. 'You knew even then that he was the –'

'You knew even then,' insisted Olive, 'that the murderer was –'

Father Brown nodded gravely. 'Yes,' he said. 'I knew even then that the murderer was old Dyke.'

'Was *who*?' repeated the Inspector and stopped amid a dead silence; punctuated only by the occasional pipe of birds.

'I mean Mr Dyke, the solicitor,' explained Father Brown, like one explaining something elementary to an infant class. 'That gentleman with grey hair who's supposed to be going to read the will.'

They all stood like statues staring at him, as he carefully filled his pipe again and struck a match. At last Burns rallied his vocal powers to break the strangling silence with an effort resembling violence.

'But, in the name of heaven, *why*?'

'Ah, why?' said the priest and rose thoughtfully, puffing at his pipe. 'As to why he did it . . . Well, I suppose the time has come to tell you, or those of you who don't know, the fact that is the key of all this business. It's a great calamity; and it's a great crime; but it's not the murder of Admiral Craven.'

He looked Olive full in the face and said very seriously:

'I tell you the bad news bluntly and in few words; because I think you are brave enough, and perhaps happy enough, to take it well. You have the chance, and I think the power, to be something like a great woman. You are not a great heiress.'

Amid the silence that followed it was he who resumed his explanation.

'Most of your father's money, I am sorry to say, has gone. It went by the financial dexterity of the grey-haired gentleman named Dyke, who is (I grieve to say) a swindler. Admiral Craven was murdered to silence him about the way in which he was swindled. The fact that he was ruined and you were disinherited is the single simple clue, not only to the murder, but to all the other mysteries in this business.' He took a puff or two and then continued.

'I told Mr Rook you were disinherited and he rushed back to help you. Mr Rook is a rather remarkable person.'

'Oh, chuck it,' said Mr Rook with a hostile air.

'Mr Rook is a monster,' said Father Brown with scientific calm. 'He is an anachronism, an atavism, a brute survival of the Stone Age. If there was one barbarous superstition we all supposed to be utterly extinct and dead in these days, it was that notion about honour and independence. But then I get mixed up with so many dead superstitions. Mr Rook is an extinct animal. He is a plesiosaurus. He did not want to live on his wife or have a wife who could call him a fortune-hunter. Therefore he sulked in a grotesque manner and only came to life again when I brought him the good news that you were ruined. He wanted to work for his wife and not be kept by her. Disgusting, isn't it? Let us turn to the brighter topic of Mr Harker.

'I told Mr Harker you were disinherited and he rushed away in a sort of panic. Do not be too hard on Mr Harker. He really had better as well as worse enthusiasms; but he had them all mixed up. There is no harm in having ambitions; but he had ambitions and called them ideals. The old sense of honour taught men to suspect success; to say, "This is a benefit; it may be a bribe". The new nine-times-accursed nonsense about Making Good teaches men to identify being good with making money. That was all that was the matter with him; in every other way he was a thoroughly good fellow, and there are thousands like him. Gazing at the stars and rising in the world were all Uplift. Marrying a good wife and marrying a rich wife were all Making Good. But he was not a cynical scoundrel; or he would simply have come back and jilted or cut you as the case might be. He could not face you; while you were there, half of his broken ideal was left.

'I did not tell the Admiral; but somebody did. Word came to him somehow, during the last grand parade on board, that his friend the family lawyer had betrayed him. He was in such a towering passion that he did what he could never have done in his senses; came straight on shore in his cocked hat and gold lace to catch the criminal; he wired to the police station, and that was why the Inspector was wandering round the Green Man. Lieutenant Rook followed him on shore because he suspected some family trouble and had half a hope he might help and put himself right. Hence his hesitating behaviour. As for his drawing his sword when he dropped behind and thought he was alone, well that's a matter of imagination. He was a romantic person who had dreamed of swords and run away to sea; and found himself in a service where he wasn't even allowed to wear a sword except about once in three years. He thought he was quite alone on the sands where he played as a boy. If you don't understand what he did, I can only say, like Stevenson, "you will never be a pirate". Also you will never be a poet; and you have never been a boy.'

'I never have,' answered Olive gravely, 'and yet I think I understand.'

'Almost every man,' continued the priest musing, 'will play with anything shaped like a sword or dagger, even if it is a paper-knife. That is why I thought it so odd when the lawyer didn't.'

'What do you mean?' asked Burns, 'didn't what?'

'Why, didn't you notice,' answered Brown, 'at that first meeting in the office, the lawyer played with a pen and not with a paper-knife; though he had a beautiful bright steel paper-knife in the pattern of a stiletto? The pens were dusty and splashed with ink; but the knife had just been cleaned. But he did not play with it. There are limits to the irony of assassins.'

After a silence the Inspector said, like one waking from a dream: 'Look here . . . I don't know whether I'm on my head or my heels; I don't know whether you think you've got to the end; but I haven't got to the beginning. Where do you get all this lawyer stuff from? What started you out on that trail?'

Father Brown laughed curtly and without mirth.

'The murderer made a slip at the start,' he said, 'and I can't think why nobody else noticed it. When you brought the first news of the death to the solicitor's office, nobody was supposed to know anything there, except that the Admiral was expected home. When you said he was drowned, I asked when it happened and Mr Dyke asked where the corpse was found.'

He paused a moment to knock out his pipe and resumed reflectively:

'Now when you are simply told of a seaman, returning from the sea, that he has been drowned, it is natural to assume that he has been drowned at sea. At any rate, to allow that he may have been drowned at sea. If he had been washed overboard, or gone down with his ship, or had his body "committed to the deep", there would be no reason to expect his body to be found at all. The moment that man asked where it was found, I was sure he knew where it was found. Because he had put it there. Nobody but the murderer need have thought of anything so unlikely as a seaman being drowned in a land-locked pool a few hundred yards from the sea. That is why I suddenly felt sick and turned green, I dare say; as green as the Green Man. I never *can* get used to finding myself suddenly sitting beside a murderer. So I had to turn it off by talking in parables; but the parable meant something, after all. I said that the body was covered with green scum, but it might just as well have been seaweed.'

It is fortunate that tragedy can never kill comedy and that the two can run side by side; and that while the only acting partner of the business of Messrs Willis, Hardman and Dyke blew his brains out when the Inspector entered the house to arrest him, Olive and Roger were calling to each other across the sands at evening, as they did when they were children together.

THE MAN WITH TWO BEARDS

This tale was told by Father Brown to Professor Crake, the celebrated criminologist, after dinner at a club, where the two were introduced to each other as sharing a harmless hobby of murder and robbery. But, as Father Brown's version rather minimized his own part in the matter, it is here retold in a more impartial style. It arose out of a playful passage of arms, in which the professor was very scientific and the priest rather sceptical.

'My good sir,' said the professor in remonstrance, 'don't you believe that criminology is a science?'

'I'm not sure,' replied Father Brown. 'Do you believe that hagiology is a science?'

'What's that?' asked the specialist sharply.

'No; it's not the study of hags, and has nothing to do with burning witches,' said the priest, smiling. 'It's the study of holy things, saints and so on. You see, the Dark Ages tried to make a science about good people. But our own humane and enlightened age is only interested in a science about bad ones. Yet I think our general experience is that every conceivable sort of man has been a saint. And I suspect you will find, too, that every conceivable sort of man has been a murderer.'

'Well, we believe murderers can be pretty well classified,' observed Crake. 'The list sounds rather long and dull; but I think it's exhaustive. First, all killing can be divided into rational and irrational, and we'll take the last first, because they are much fewer. There is such a thing as homicidal mania, or love of butchery in the abstract. There is such a thing as irrational antipathy, though it's very seldom homicidal. Then we come to the true motives: of these, some are less rational in the sense of being merely romantic and retrospective. Acts of pure revenge are acts of hopeless revenge. Thus a lover will sometimes kill a rival he could never supplant, or a rebel assassinate a tyrant after the conquest is complete. But, more often, even these acts have a rational explanation. They are hopeful murders. They fall into the larger section of the second division, of what we may call prudential crimes. These, again, fall chiefly under two descriptions. A man kills either in order to obtain what the other man possesses, either by theft or inheritance, or to stop the other man from acting in some way: as in the case of killing a blackmailer or a political opponent; or, in the case of a rather more passive obstacle, a husband or wife whose continued functioning, as such, interferes with other things. We believe that classification is pretty thoroughly thought out and, properly applied, covers the whole ground. But I'm afraid that it perhaps sounds rather dull; I hope I'm not boring you.'

'Not at all,' said Father Brown. 'If I seemed a little absent-minded I must apologize; the truth is, I was thinking of a man I once knew. He was a murderer; but I can't see where he fits into your museum of murderers. He was not mad, nor did he like killing. He did not hate the man he killed; he hardly knew him, and certainly had nothing to avenge on him. The other man did not possess anything that he could possibly want. The other man was not behaving in any way which the murderer wanted to stop. The murdered man was not in a position to hurt, or hinder, or even affect the murderer in any way. There was no woman in the case. There were no politics in the case. This man killed a fellow-creature who was practically a stranger, and that for a very strange reason; which is possibly unique in human history.'

And so, in his own more conversational fashion, he told the story. The story may well begin in a sufficiently respectable setting, at the breakfast table of a worthy though wealthy suburban family named Bankes, where the normal discussion of the newspaper had, for once, been silenced by the discussion about a mystery nearer home. Such people are sometimes accused of gossip about their neighbours, but they are in that matter almost inhumanly innocent. Rustic villagers tell tales about their neighbours, true and false; but the curious culture of the modern suburb will believe anything it is told in the papers about the wickedness of the Pope, or the martyrdom of the King of the Cannibal Islands, and, in the excitement of these topics, never knows what is happening next door. In this case, however, the two forms of interest actually coincided in a coincidence of thrilling intensity. Their own suburb had actually been mentioned in their favourite newspaper. It seemed to them like a new proof of their own existence when they saw the name in print. It was almost as if they had been unconscious and invisible before; and now they were as real as the King of the Cannibal Islands.

It was stated in the paper that a once-famous criminal, known as Michael Moonshine, and many other names that were presumably not his own, had recently been released after a long term of imprisonment for his numerous burglaries; that his whereabouts were being kept quiet, but that he was believed to have settled down in the suburb in question, which we will call for convenience Chisham. A résumé of some of his famous and daring exploits and escapes was given in the same issue. For it is a character of that kind of press, intended for that kind of public, that it assumes that its readers have no memories. While the peasant will remember an outlaw like Robin Hood or Rob Roy for centuries, the clerk will hardly remember the name of the criminal about whom he argued in trams and tubes two years before. Yet, Michael Moonshine had really shown some of the heroic rascality of Rob Roy or Robin Hood. He was worthy to be turned into legend and not merely into news. He was far too capable a burglar to be a murderer. But his terrific strength and the ease with which he knocked policemen over like ninepins, stunned people, and bound and gagged them, gave something almost like a final touch of fear or mystery to the fact that he never killed them. People almost felt that he would have been more human if he had.

Mr Simon Bankes, the father of the family, was at once better read and more old-fashioned than the rest. He was a sturdy man, with a short grey beard and a brow barred with wrinkles. He had a turn for anecdotes and reminiscence, and he distinctly remembered the days when Londoners had lain awake listening for Mike Moonshine as they did for Springheeled Jack. Then there was his wife, a thin, dark lady. There was a sort of acid elegance about her, for her family had much more money than her husband's, if rather less education; and she even possessed a very valuable emerald necklace upstairs, that gave her a right to prominence in a discussion about thieves. There was his daughter, Opal, who was also thin and dark and supposed to be psychic – at any rate, by herself; for she had little domestic encouragement. Spirits of an ardently astral turn will be well advised not to materialize as members of a large family. There was her brother John, a burly youth, particularly boisterous in his indifference to her spiritual development; and otherwise distinguishable only by his interest in motor-cars. He seemed to be always in the act of selling one car and buying another; and by some process, hard for the economic theorist to follow, it was always possible to buy a much better article by selling the one that was damaged or discredited. There was his brother Philip, a young man with dark curly hair, distinguished by his attention to dress; which is doubtless part of the duty of a stockbroker's clerk, but, as the stockbroker was prone to hint, hardly the whole of it. Finally, there was present at this family scene his friend, Daniel Devine, who was also dark and exquisitely dressed, but bearded in a fashion that was somewhat foreign, and therefore, for many, slightly menacing.

It was Devine who had introduced the topic of the newspaper paragraph, tactfully insinuating so effective an instrument of distraction at what looked like the beginning of a small family quarrel; for the psychic lady had begun the description of a vision she had had of pale faces floating in empty night outside her window, and

John Bankes was trying to roar down this revelation of a higher state with more than his usual heartiness.

But the newspaper reference to their new and possibly alarming neighbour soon put both controversialists out of court.

'How frightful,' cried Mrs Bankes. 'He must be quite a newcomer; but who can he possibly be?'

'I don't know any particularly newcomers,' said her husband, 'except Sir Leopold Pulman, at Beechwood House.'

'My dear,' said the lady, 'how absurd you are – Sir Leopold!' Then, after a pause, she added: 'If anybody suggested his secretary now – that man with the whiskers; I've always said, ever since he got the place Philip ought to have had –'

'Nothing doing,' said Philip languidly, making his sole contribution to the conversation. 'Not good enough.'

'The only one I know,' observed Devine, 'is that man called Carver, who is stopping at Smith's Farm. He lives a very quiet life, but he's quite interesting to talk to. I think John has had some business with him.'

'Knows a bit about cars,' conceded the monomaniac John. 'He'll know a bit more when he's been in my new car.'

Devine smiled slightly; everybody had been threatened with the hospitality of John's new car. Then he added reflectively:

'That's a little what I feel about him. He knows a lot about motoring and travelling, and the active ways of the world, and yet he always stays at home pottering about round old Smith's beehives. Says he's only interested in bee culture, and that's why he's staying with Smith. It seems a very quiet hobby for a man of his sort. However, I've no doubt John's car will shake him up a bit.'

As Devine walked away from the house that evening his dark face wore an expression of concentrated thought. His thoughts would, perhaps, have been worthy of our attention, even at this stage; but it is enough to say that their practical upshot was a resolution to pay an immediate visit to Mr Carver at the house of Mr Smith. As he was making his way thither he encountered Barnard, the secretary at Beechwood House, conspicuous by his lanky figure and the large side whiskers which Mrs Bankes counted among her private wrongs. Their acquaintance was slight, and their conversation brief and casual; but Devine seemed to find in it food for further cogitation.

'Look here,' he said abruptly, 'excuse my asking, but is it true that Lady Pulman has some very famous jewellery up at the House? I'm not a professional thief, but I've just heard there's one hanging about.'

'I'll get her to give an eye to them,' answered the secretary. 'To tell the truth, I've ventured to warn her about them already myself. I hope she has attended to it.'

As they spoke, there came the hideous cry of a motor-horn just behind, and John Bankes came to a stop beside them, radiant at his own steering-wheel. When he heard of Devine's destination he claimed it as his own, though his tone suggested rather an abstract relish for offering people a ride. The ride was consumed in continuous praises of the car, now mostly in the matter of its adaptability to weather.

'Shuts up as tight as a box,' he said, 'and opens as easy – as easy as opening your mouth.'

Devine's mouth, at the moment, did not seem so easy to open, and they arrived at Smith's farm to the sound of a soliloquy. Passing the outer gate, Devine found the man he was looking for without going into the house. The man was walking about in the garden, with his hands in his pockets, wearing a large, limp straw hat; a man with a long face and a large chin. The wide brim cut off the upper part of his face with a shadow that looked a little like a mask. In the background was a row of sunny beehives, along which an elderly man, presumably Mr Smith, was moving accompanied by a short, commonplace-looking companion in black clerical costume.

'I say,' burst in the irrepressible John, before Devine could offer any polite greeting, 'I've brought her round to give you a little run. You see if she isn't better than a "Thunder-bolt".'

Mr Carver's mouth set into a smile that may have been meant to be gracious, but looked rather grim. 'I'm afraid I shall be too busy for pleasure this evening,' he said.

'How doth the little busy bee,' observed Devine, equally enigmatically. 'Your bees must be very busy if they keep you at it all night. I was wondering if –'

'Well,' demanded Carver, with a certain cool defiance.

'Well, they say we should make hay while the sun shines,' said Devine. 'Perhaps you make honey while the moon shines.'

There came a flash from the shadow of the broad-brimmed hat, as the whites of the man's eyes shifted and shone.

'Perhaps there is a good deal of moonshine in the

business,' he said: 'but I warn you my bees do not only make honey. They sting.'

'*Are* you coming along in the car?' insisted the staring John. But Carver, though he threw off the momentary air of sinister significance with which he had been answering Devine, was still positive in his polite refusal.

'I can't possibly go,' he said. 'Got a lot of writing to do. Perhaps you'd be kind enough to give some of my friends a run, if you want a companion. This is my friend, Mr Smith, Father Brown.'

'Of course,' cried Bankes; 'let 'em all come.'

'Thank you very much,' said Father Brown. 'I'm afraid I shall have to decline; I've got to go on to Benediction in a few minutes.'

'Mr Smith is your man, then,' said Carver, with something almost like impatience. 'I'm sure Smith is longing for a motor ride.'

Smith, who wore a broad grin, bore no appearance of longing for anything. He was an active little old man with a very honest wig; one of those wigs that look no more natural than a hat. Its tinge of yellow was out of keeping with his colourless complexion. He shook his head and answered with amiable obstinacy:

'I remember I went over this road ten years ago – in one of those contraptions. Came over in it from my sister's place at Holmgate, and never been over that road in a car since. It was rough going I can tell you.'

'Ten years ago!' scoffed John Bankes. 'Two thousand years ago you went in an ox wagon. Do you think cars haven't changed in ten years – and roads, too, for that matter? In my little bus you don't know the wheels are going round. You think you're just flying.'

'I'm sure Smith wants to go flying,' urged Carver. 'It's the dream of his life. Come, Smith, go over to Holmgate and see your sister. You know you ought to go and see your sister. Go over and stay the night if you like.'

'Well, I generally walk over, so I generally do stay the night,' said old Smith. 'No need to trouble the gentleman today, particularly.'

'But think what fun it will be for your sister to see you arrive in a car!' cried Carver. 'You really ought to go. Don't be so selfish.'

'That's it,' assented Bankes, with buoyant benevolence. 'Don't you be selfish. It won't hurt you. You aren't afraid of it, are you?'

'Well,' said Mr Smith, blinking thoughtfully, 'I don't want to be selfish, and I don't think I'm afraid. I'll come with you if you put it that way.'

The pair drove off, amid waving salutations that seemed somehow to give the little group the appearance of a cheering crowd. Yet Devine and the priest only joined in out of courtesy, and they both felt it was the dominating gesture of their host that gave it its final air of farewell. The detail gave them a curious sense of the pervasive force of his personality.

The moment the car was out of sight he turned to them with a sort of boisterous apology and said: 'Well!'

He said it with that curious heartiness which is the reverse of hospitality. That extreme geniality is the same as a dismissal.

'I must be going,' said Devine. 'We must not interrupt the busy bee. I'm afraid I know very little about bees; sometimes I can hardly tell a bee from a wasp.'

'I've kept wasps, too,' answered the mysterious Mr Carver.

When his guests were a few yards down the street, Devine said rather impulsively to his companion: 'Rather an odd scene that, don't you think?'

'Yes,' replied Father Brown. 'And what do you think about it?'

Devine looked at the little man in black, and something in the gaze of his great, grey eyes seemed to renew his impulse.

'I think,' he said, 'that Carver was very anxious to have the house to himself tonight. I don't know whether you had any such suspicions?'

'I may have my suspicions,' replied the priest, 'but I'm not sure whether they're the same as yours.'

That evening, when the last dusk was turning into dark in the gardens round the family mansion, Opal Bankes was moving through some of the dim and empty rooms with even more than her usual abstraction; and anyone who had looked at her closely would have noted that her pale face had more than its usual pallor. Despite its bourgeois luxury, the house as a whole had a rather unique shade of melancholy. It was the sort of immediate sadness that belongs to things that are old rather than ancient. It was full of faded fashions, rather than historic customs; of the order and ornament that is just recent enough to be recognized as dead. Here and there, Early Victorian coloured glass tinted the twilight; the high ceilings made the long rooms look narrow; and at the end of the long room down which she was walking was one of those round windows, to be found in the buildings of its period. As she came to about the middle of the room, she stopped, and then suddenly swayed a little, as if some invisible hand had struck her on the face.

An instant after there was the noise of knocking on the front door, dulled by the closed doors between. She knew that the rest of the household were in the upper parts of the house, but she could not have analysed the motive that made her go to the front door herself. On the doorstep stood a dumpy and dingy figure in black, which she recognized as the Roman Catholic priest, whose name was Brown. She knew him only slightly; but she liked him. He did not encourage her psychic views; quite the contrary; but he discouraged them as if they mattered and not as if they did not matter. It was not so much that he did not sympathize with her opinions, as that he did sympathize but did not agree. All this was in some sort of chaos in her mind as she found herself saying, without greeting, or waiting to hear his business:

'I'm so glad you've come. I've seen a ghost.'

'There's no need to be distressed about that,' he said. 'It often happens. Most of the ghosts aren't ghosts, and the few that may be won't do you any harm. Was it any ghost in particular?'

'No,' she admitted, with a vague feeling of relief, 'it wasn't so much the thing itself as an atmosphere of awful decay, a sort of luminous ruin. It was a face. A face at the window. But it was pale and goggling, and looked like the picture of Judas.'

'Well, some people do look like that,' reflected the priest, 'and I dare say they look in at windows, sometimes. May I come in and see where it happened?'

When she returned to the room with the visitor, however, other members of the family had assembled, and those of a less psychic habit had thought it convenient to light the lamps. In the presence of Mrs Bankes, Father Brown assumed a more conventional civility, and apologized for his intrusion.

'I'm afraid it is taking a liberty with your house, Mrs Bankes,' he said. 'But I think I can explain how the business happens to concern you. I was up at the Pulmans' place just now, when I was rung up and asked to come round here to meet a man who is coming to communicate something that may be of some moment to you. I should not have added myself to the party, only I am wanted, apparently, because I am a witness to what has happened up at Beechwood. In fact, it was I who had to give the alarm.'

'What has happened?' repeated the lady.

'There has been a robbery up at Beechwood House,' said Father Brown, gravely; 'a robbery, and what I fear is worse, Lady Pulman's jewels have gone; and her unfortunate secretary, Mr Barnard, was picked up in the garden, having evidently been shot by the escaping burglar.'

'That man,' ejaculated the lady of the house. 'I believe he was –'

She encountered the grave gaze of the priest, and her words suddenly went from her; she never knew why.

'I communicated with the police,' he went on, 'and with another authority interested in this case; and they say that even a superficial examination has revealed footprints and fingerprints and other indications of a wellknown criminal.'

At this point, the conference was for a moment disturbed by the return of John Bankes, from what appeared to be an abortive expedition in the car. Old Smith seemed to have been a disappointing passenger, after all.

'Funked it, after all, at the last minute,' he announced with noisy disgust. 'Bolted off while I was looking at what I thought was a puncture. Last time I'll take one of these yokels –'

But his complaints received small attention in the general excitement that gathered round Father Brown and his news.

'Somebody will arrive in a moment,' went on the priest, with the same air of weighty reserve, 'who will relieve me of this responsibility. When I have confronted you with him I shall have done my duty as a witness in a serious business. It only remains for me to say that a servant up at Beechwood House told me that she had seen a face at one of the windows –'

'I saw a face,' said Opal, 'at one of our windows.'

'Oh, you are always seeing faces,' said her brother John roughly.

'It is as well to see facts even if they are faces,' said Father Brown equably, 'and I think the face you saw –'

Another knock at the front door sounded through the house, and a minute afterwards the door of the room opened and another figure appeared. Devine half-rose from his chair at the sight of it.

It was a tall, erect figure, with a long, rather cadaverous face, ending in a formidable chin. The brow was rather bald, and the eyes bright and blue, which Devine had last seen obscured with a broad straw hat.

'Pray don't let anybody move,' said the man called Carver, in clear and courteous tones. But to Devine's disturbed mind the courtesy had an ominous resemblance to that of a brigand who holds a company motionless with a pistol.

'Please sit down, Mr Devine,' said Carver; 'and, with Mrs Bankes's permission, I will follow your example. My presence here necessitates an explanation. I rather fancy you suspected me of being an eminent and distinguished burglar.'

'I did,' said Devine grimly.

'As you remarked,' said Carver, 'it is not always easy to know a wasp from a bee.'

After a pause, he continued: 'I can claim to be one of the more useful, though equally annoying, insects. I am a detective, and I have come down to investigate an alleged renewal of the activities of the criminal calling himself Michael Moonshine. Jewel robberies were his speciality; and there has just been one of them at Beechwood House, which, by all the technical tests, is obviously his work. Not only do the prints correspond, but you may possibly know that when he was last arrested, and it is believed on other occasions also, he wore a simple but effective disguise of a red beard and a pair of large horn-rimmed spectacles.'

Opal Bankes leaned forward fiercely.

'That was it,' she cried in excitement, 'that was the face I saw, with great goggles and a red, ragged beard like Judas. I thought it was a ghost.'

'That was also the ghost the servant at Beechwood saw,' said Carver dryly.

He laid some papers and packages on the table, and began carefully to unfold them. 'As I say,' he continued, 'I was sent down here to make inquiries about the criminal plans of this man, Moonshine. That is why I interested myself in bee-keeping and went to stay with Mr Smith.'

There was a silence, and then Devine started and spoke: 'You don't seriously mean to say that nice old man –'

'Come, Mr Devine,' said Carver, with a smile, 'you believed a beehive was only a hiding-place for me. Why shouldn't it be a hiding-place for him?'

Devine nodded gloomily, and the detective turned back to his papers. 'Suspecting Smith, I wanted to get him out of the way and go through his belongings; so I took advantage of Mr Bankes's kindness in giving him a joy ride. Searching his house, I found some curious things to be owned by an innocent old rustic interested only in bees. This is one of them.'

From the unfolded paper he lifted a long, hairy object almost scarlet in colour – the sort of sham beard that is worn in theatricals.

Beside it lay an old pair of heavy horn-rimmed spectacles.

'But I also found something,' continued Carver, 'that more directly concerns this house, and must be my excuse for intruding tonight. I found a memorandum, with notes of the names and conjectural value of various pieces of jewellery in the neighbourhood. Immediately after the note of Lady Pulman's tiara was the mention of an emerald necklace belonging to Mrs Bankes.'

Mrs Bankes, who had hitherto regarded the invasion of her house with an air of supercilious bewilderment, suddenly grew attentive. Her face suddenly looked ten years older and much more intelligent. But before she could speak the impetuous John had risen to his full height like a trumpeting elephant.

'And the tiara's gone already,' he roared; 'and the necklace – I'm going to see about that necklace!'

'Not a bad idea,' said Carver, as the young man rushed from the room; 'though, of course, we've been keeping our eyes open since we've been here. Well, it took me a little time to make out the memorandum, which was in cipher, and Father Brown's telephone message from the House came as I was near the end. I asked him to run round here first with the news, and I would follow; and so –'

His speech was sundered by a scream. Opal was standing up and pointing rigidly at the round window.

'There it is again!' she cried.

For a moment they all saw something – something that cleared the lady of the charges of lying and hysteria not uncommonly brought against her. Thrust out of the slate-blue darkness without, the face was pale, or, perhaps, blanched by pressure against the glass; and the great glaring eyes, encircled as with rings, gave it rather the look of a great fish out of the dark-blue sea nosing at the porthole of a ship. But the gills or fins of the fish were a coppery red; they were, in truth, fierce red whiskers and the upper part of a red beard. The next moment it had vanished.

Devine had taken a single stride towards the window when a shout resounded through the house, a shout that seemed to shake it. It seemed almost too deafening to be distinguishable as words; yet it was enough to stop Devine in his stride, and he knew what had happened.

'Necklace gone!' shouted John Bankes, appearing huge and heaving in the doorway, and almost instantly vanishing again with the plunge of a pursuing hound.

'Thief was at the window just now!' cried the detective, who had already darted to the door, following the head-long John, who was already in the garden.

'Be careful,' wailed the lady, 'they have pistols and things.'

'So have I,' boomed the distant voice of the dauntless John out of the dark garden.

Devine had, indeed, noticed as the young man plunged past him that he was defiantly brandishing a revolver, and hoped there would be no need for him to so defend himself. But even as he had the thought, came the shock of two shots, as if one answered the other, and awakened a wild flock of echoes in that still suburban garden. They flapped into silence.

'Is John dead?' asked Opal in a low, shuddering voice.

Father Brown had already advanced deeper into the darkness, and stood with his back to them, looking down at something. It was he who answered her.

'No,' he said; 'it is the other.'

Carver had joined him, and for a moment the two figures, the tall and the short, blocked out what view the fitful and stormy moonlight would allow. Then they moved to one side, and the others saw the small, wiry figure lying slightly twisted, as if with its last struggle. The false red beard was thrust upwards, as if scornfully at the sky, and the moon shone on the great sham spectacles of the man who had been called Moonshine.

'What an end,' muttered the detective, Carver. 'After all his adventures to be shot almost by accident by a stockbroker in a suburban garden.'

The stockbroker himself naturally regarded his own

triumph with more solemnity, though not without nervousness.

'I had to do it,' he gasped, still panting with exertion. 'I'm sorry, he fired at me.'

'There will have to be an inquest, of course,' said Carver, gravely. 'But I think there will be nothing for you to worry about. There's a revolver fallen from his hand with one shot discharged; and he certainly didn't fire after he'd got yours.'

By this time they had assembled again in the room, and the detective was getting his papers together for departure. Father Brown was standing opposite to him, looking down at the table, as if in a brown study. Then he spoke abruptly:

'Mr Carver, you have certainly worked out a very complete case in a very masterly way. I rather suspected your professional business; but I never guessed you would link everything up together so quickly – the bees and the beard and the spectacles and the cipher and the necklace and everything.'

'Always satisfactory to get a case really rounded off,' said Carver.

'Yes,' said Father Brown, still looking at the table. 'I admire it very much.' Then he added with a modesty verging on nervousness: 'It's only fair to you to say that I don't believe a word of it.'

Devine leaned forward with sudden interest. 'Do you mean you don't believe he is Moonshine, the burglar?'

'I know he is the burglar, but he didn't burgle,' answered Father Brown. 'I know he didn't come here, or to the great house, to steal jewels, or get shot getting away with them. Where are the jewels?'

'Where they generally are in such cases,' said Carver. 'He's either hidden them or passed them on to a confederate. This was not a one-man job. Of course, my people are searching the garden and warning the district.'

'Perhaps,' suggested Mrs Bankes, 'the confederate stole the necklace while Moonshine was looking in at the window.'

'Why was Moonshine looking in at the window?' asked Father Brown quietly. 'Why should he want to look in at the window?'

'Well, what do you think?' cried the cheery John.

'I think,' said Father Brown, 'that he never did want to look in at the window.'

'Then why did he do it?' demanded Carver. 'What's the good of talking in the air like that? We've seen the whole thing acted before our very eyes.'

'I've seen a good many things acted before my very eyes that I didn't believe in,' replied the priest. 'So have you, on the stage and off.'

'Father Brown,' said Devine, with a certain respect in his tones, 'will you tell us why you can't believe your eyes?'

'Yes, I will try to tell you,' answered the priest. Then he said gently: 'You know what I am and what we are. We don't bother you much. We try to be friends with all our neighbours. But you can't think we do nothing. You can't think we know nothing. We mind our own business; but we know our own people. I knew this dead man very well indeed; I was his confessor, and his friend. So far as a man can, I knew his mind when he left that garden today; and his mind was like a glass hive full of golden bees. It's an understatement to say his reformation was sincere. He was one of those great penitents who manage to make more out of penitence than others can make out of virtue. I say I was his confessor; but, indeed, it was I who went to him for comfort. It did me good to be near so good a man. And when I saw him lying there dead in the garden, it seemed to me as if certain strange words that were said of old were spoken over him aloud in my ear. They might well be; for if ever a man went straight to heaven, it might be he.'

'Hang it all,' said John Bankes restlessly, 'after all, he was a convicted thief.'

'Yes,' said Father Brown; 'and only a convicted thief has ever in this world heard that assurance: "This night shalt thou be with Me in Paradise".'

Nobody seemed to know what to do with the silence that followed, until Devine said, abruptly, at last:

'Then how in the world would you explain it all?'

The priest shook his head. 'I can't explain it at all, just yet,' he said, simply. 'I can see one or two odd things, but I don't understand them. As yet I've nothing to go on to prove the man's innocence, except the man. But I'm quite sure I'm right.'

He sighed, and put out his hand for his big, black hat. As he removed it he remained gazing at the table with rather a new expression, his round, straight-haired head cocked at a new angle. It was rather as if some curious animal had come out of his hat, as out of the hat of a conjurer. But the others, looking at the table, could see nothing there but the detective's documents and the tawdry old property beard and spetacles.

'Lord bless us,' muttered Father Brown, 'and he's lying

outside dead, in a beard and spectacles.' He swung round suddenly upon Devine. 'Here's something to follow up, if you want to know. *Why did he have two beards?*'

With that he bustled in his undignified way out of the room; but Devine was now devoured with curiosity, and pursued him into the front garden.

'I can't tell you now,' said Father Brown. 'I'm not sure, and I'm bothered about what to do. Come round and see me tomorrow, and I may be able to tell you the whole thing. It may already be settled for me, and – did you hear that noise?'

'A motor car starting,' remarked Devine.

'Mr John Bankes's motor car,' said the priest. 'I believe it goes very fast.'

'He certainly is of that opinion,' said Devine, with a smile.

'It will go far, as well as fast, tonight,' said Father Brown.

'And what do you mean by that?' demanded the other.

'I mean it will not return,' replied the priest. 'John Bankes suspected something of what I knew from what I said. John Bankes has gone and the emeralds and all the other jewels with him.'

Next day, Devine found Father Brown moving to and fro in front of the row of beehives, sadly, but with a certain serenity.

'I've been telling the bees,' he said. 'You know one has to tell the bees! "Those singing masons building roofs of gold." What a line!' Then more abruptly. 'He would like the bees looked after.'

'I hope he doesn't want the human beings neglected,

when the whole swarm is buzzing with curiosity,' observed the young man. 'You were quite right when you said that Bankes was gone with the jewels; but I don't know how you knew, or even what there was to be known.'

Father Brown blinked benevolently at the beehives and said:

'One sort of stumbles on things, and there was one stumbling-block at the start. I was puzzled by poor Barnard being shot up at Beechwood House. Now, even when Michael was a master criminal, he made it a point of honour, even a point of vanity, to succeed without any killing. It seemed extraordinary that when he had become a sort of saint he should go out of his way to commit the sin he had despised when he was a sinner. The rest of the business puzzled me to the last; I could make nothing out of it, except that it wasn't true. Then I had a belated gleam of sense when I saw the beard and goggles and remembered the thief had come in another beard with other goggles. Now, of course, it was just possible that he had duplicates; but it was at least a coincidence that he used neither the old glasses nor the old beard, both in good repair. Again, it was just possible that he went out without them and had to procure new ones; but it was unlikely. There was nothing to make him go motoring with Bankes at all; if he was really going burgling, he could have taken his outfit easily in his pocket. Besides, beards don't grow on bushes. He would have found it hard to get such things anywhere in the time.

'No, the more I thought of it the more I felt there was something funny about his having a completely new outfit. And then the truth began to dawn on me by reason, which I knew already by instinct. He never did go out with Bankes with any intention of putting on the disguise. He never did put on the disguise. Somebody else manufactured the disguise at leisure, and then put it on him.'

'Put it on him!' repeated Devine. 'How the devil could they?'

'Let us go back,' said Father Brown, 'and look at the thing through another window – the window through which the young lady saw the ghost.'

'The ghost!' repeated the other, with a slight start.

'She called it the ghost,' said the little man, with composure, 'and perhaps she was not so far wrong. It's quite true that she is what they call psychic. Her only mistake is in thinking that being psychic is being spiritual. Some animals are psychic; anyhow, she is a sensitive, and she was right when she felt that the face at the window had a sort of horrible halo of deathly things.'

'You mean –' began Devine.

'I mean it was a dead man who looked in at the window,' said Father Brown. 'It was a dead man who crawled round more than one house, looking in at more than one window. Creepy, wasn't it? But in one way it was the reverse of a ghost; for it was not the antic of the soul freed from the body. It was the antic of the body freed from the soul.'

He blinked again at the beehive and continued: 'But, I suppose, the shortest explanation is to take it from the standpoint of the man who did it. You know the man who did it. John Bankes.'

'The very last man I should have thought of,' said Devine.

'The very first man I thought of,' said Father Brown; 'in so far as I had any right to think of anybody. My friend, there are no good or bad social types or trades. Any man can be a murderer like poor John; any man, even the same man, can be a saint like poor Michael. But if there is one type that tends at times to be more utterly godless than another, it is that rather brutal sort of business man. He has no social ideal, let alone religion; he has neither the gentleman's traditions nor the trade unionist's class loyalty. All his boasts about getting good bargains were practically boasts of having cheated people. His snubbing of his sister's poor little attempts at mysticism was detestable. Her mysticism was all nonsense; but he only hated spiritualism because it was spirituality. Anyhow, there's no doubt he was the villain of the piece; the only interest is in a rather original piece of villainy. It was really a new and unique motive for murder. It was the motive of using the corpse as a stage property – a sort of hideous doll or dummy. At the start he conceived a plan of killing Michael in the motor, merely to take him home and pretend to have killed him in the garden. But all sorts of fantastic finishing touches followed quite naturally from the primary fact; that he had at his disposal in a closed car at night the dead body of a recognized and recognizable burglar. He could leave his fingerprints and footprints; he could lean the familiar face against windows and take it away. You will notice that Moonshine ostensibly appeared and vanished while Bankes was ostensibly out of the room looking for the emerald necklace.

'Finally, he had only to tumble the corpse on to the lawn, fire a shot from each pistol, and there he was. It might never have been found out but for a guess about the two beards.'

'Why had your friend Michael kept the old beard?' Devine said thoughtfully. 'That seems to me questionable.'

'To me, who knew him, it seems quite inevitable,' replied Father Brown. 'His whole attitude was like that wig that he wore. There was no disguise about his disguises. He didn't want the old disguise any more, but he wasn't frightened of it; he would have felt it false to destroy the false beard. It would have been like hiding; and he was not hiding. He was not hiding from God; he was not hiding from himself. He was in the broad daylight. If they'd taken him back to prison, he'd still have been quite happy. He was not whitewashed, but washed white. There was something very strange about him; almost as strange as the grotesque dance of death through which he was dragged after he was dead. When he moved to and fro smiling among these beehives, even then, in a most radiant and shining sense, he was dead. He was out of the judgement of this world.'

There was a short pause, and then Devine shrugged his shoulders and said: 'It all comes back to bees and wasps looking very much alike in this world, doesn't it?'

THE SINS OF PRINCE SARADINE

When Flambeau took his month's holiday from his office in Westminster he took it in a small sailing-boat, so small that it passed much of its time as a rowing-boat. He took it, moreover, on little rivers in the Eastern counties, rivers so small that the boat looked like a magic boat sailing on land through meadows and cornfields. The vessel was just comfortable for two people; there was room only for necessities, and Flambeau had stocked it with such things as his special philosophy considered necessary. They reduced themselves, apparently, to four essentials: tins of salmon, if he should want to eat; loaded revolvers, if he should want to fight; a bottle of brandy, presumably in case he should faint; and a priest, presumably in case he should die. With this light luggage he crawled down the little Norfolk rivers, intending to reach the Broads at last, but meanwhile delighting in the over-hanging gardens and meadows, the mirrored mansions or villages, lingering to fish in the pools and corners, and in some sense hugging the shore.

Like a true philosopher, Flambeau had no aim in his holiday; but, like a true philosopher, he had an excuse. He had a sort of half purpose, which he took just so seriously that its success would crown the holiday, but just so lightly that its failure would not spoil it. Years ago, when he had been a king of thieves and the most famous figure in Paris, he had often received wild communications of approval, denunciation or even love; but one had, somehow, stuck in his memory. It consisted simply of a visiting-card, in an envelope with an English postmark. On the back of the card was written in French and in green ink: 'If you ever retire and become respectable, come and see me. I want to meet you, for I have met all the other great men of my time. That trick of yours of getting one detective to arrest the other was the most splendid scene in French history.' On the front of the card was engraved in the formal fashion, 'Prince Saradine, Reed House, Reed Island, Norfolk.'

He had not troubled much about the prince then, beyond ascertaining that he had been a brilliant and fashionable figure in southern Italy. In his youth, it was said, he had eloped with a married woman of high rank; the escapade was scarcely startling in his social world, but it had clung to men's minds because of an additional tragedy: the alleged suicide of the insulted husband, who appeared to have flung himself over a precipice in Sicily. The prince then lived in Vienna for a time, but his more recent years seemed to have been passed in perpetual and restless travel. But when Flambeau, like the prince himself, had left European celebrity and settled in England, it occurred to him that he might pay a surprise visit to this eminent exile in the Norfolk Broads. Whether he should find the place he had no idea; and, indeed, it was sufficiently small and forgotten. But, as things fell out, he found it much sooner than he expected.

They had moored their boat one night under a bank veiled in high grasses and short pollarded trees. Sleep, after heavy sculling, had come to them early, and by a corresponding accident they awoke before it was light. To speak more strictly, they awoke before it was daylight; for a large lemon moon was only just setting in the forest of high grass above their heads, and the sky was of a vivid violet-blue, nocturnal but bright. Both men had simultaneously a reminiscence of childhood, of the elfin and adventurous time when tall weeds close over us like woods. Standing up thus against the large low moon the daisies really seemed to be giant daisies, the dandelions to be giant dandelions. Somehow it reminded them of the dado of a nursery wallpaper. The drop of the river-bed sufficed to sink them under the roots of all shrubs and flowers and make them gaze upwards at the grass.

'By Jove!' said Flambeau; 'it's like being in fairyland.'

Father Brown sat bolt upright in the boat and crossed himself. His movement was so abrupt that his friend asked him, with a mild stare, what was the matter.

'The people who wrote the medieval ballads,' answered the priest, 'knew more about fairies than you do. It isn't only nice things that happen in fairyland.'

'Oh, bosh!' said Flambeau. 'Only nice things could happen under such an innocent moon. I am for pushing on now and seeing what does really come. We may die and rot before we ever see again such a moon or such a mood.'

'All right,' said Father Brown. 'I never said it was always wrong to enter fairyland. I only said it was always dangerous.'

They pushed slowly up the brightening river; the

glowing violet of the sky and the pale gold of the moon grew fainter and fainter, and faded into that vast colourless cosmos that precedes the colours of the dawn. When the first faint stripes of red and gold and grey split the horizon from end to end they were broken by the black bulk of a town or village which sat on the river just ahead of them. It was already an easy twilight, in which all things were visible, when they came under the hanging roofs and bridges of this riverside hamlet. The houses, with their long, low, stooping roofs, seemed to come down to drink at the river, like huge grey and red cattle. The broadening and whitening dawn had already turned to working daylight before they saw any living creature on the wharfs and bridges of that silent town. Eventually they saw a very placid and prosperous man in his shirt-sleeves, with a face as round as the recently sunken moon, and rays of red whisker around the low arc of it, who was leaning on a post above the sluggish tide. By an impulse not to be analysed, Flambeau rose to his full height in the swaying boat and shouted at the man to ask if he knew Reed Island or Reed House. The prosperous man's smile grew slightly more expansive, and he simply pointed up the river towards the next bend of it. Flambeau went ahead without further speech.

The boat took many such grassy corners and followed many such reedy and silent reaches of river; but before the search had become monotonous they had swung round a specially sharp angle and come into the silence of a sort of pool or lake, the sight of which instinctively arrested them. For in the middle of this wider piece of water, fringed on every side with rushes, lay a long, low islet along which ran a long, low house or bungalow built of bamboo or some kind of tough tropic cane. The up-standing rods of bamboo which made the walls were pale yellow, the sloping rods that made the roof were of darker red or brown, otherwise the long house was a thing of repetition and monotony. The early morning breeze rustled the reeds round the island and sang in the strange ribbed house as in a giant pan-pipe.

'By George!' cried Flambeau; 'here is the place, after all! Here is Reed Island, if ever there was one. Here is Reed House, if it is anywhere. I believe that fat man with whiskers was a fairy.'

'Perhaps,' remarked Father Brown impartially. 'If he was, he was a bad fairy.'

But even as he spoke the impetuous Flambeau had run his boat ashore in the rattling reeds, and they stood on the long, quaint islet beside the old and silent house.

The house stood with its back, as it were, to the river and the only landing-stage; the main entrance was on the other side, and looked down the long island garden. The visitors approached it, therefore, by a small path running round nearly three sides of the house, close under the low eaves. Through three different windows on three different sides they looked in on the same long, well-lit room, panelled in light wood, with a large number of looking-glasses, and laid out as for an elegant lunch. The front door, when they came round to it at last, was flanked by two turquoise-blue flower-pots. It was opened by a butler of the drearier type – long, lean, grey and listless – who murmured that Prince Saradine was from home at present, but was expected hourly; the house being kept ready for him and his guests. The exhibition of the card with the scrawl of green ink awoke a flicker of life in the parchment face of this depressed retainer, and it was with a certain shaky courtesy that he suggested that the strangers should remain. 'His Highness may be here any minute,' he said, 'and would be distressed to have just missed any gentleman he had invited. We have orders always to keep a little cold lunch for him and his friends, and I am sure he would wish it to be offered.'

Moved with curiosity to this minor adventure, Flambeau assented gracefully, and followed the old man, who ushered him ceremoniously into the long, lightly panelled room. There was nothing very notable about it, except the rather unusual alternation of many long, low windows with many long, low oblongs of looking-glass, which gave a singular air of lightness and unsubstantialness to the place. It was somehow like lunching out of doors. One or two pictures of a quiet kind hung in the corners: one a large grey photograph of a very young man in uniform, another a red chalk sketch of two long-haired boys. Asked by Flambeau whether the soldierly person was the prince, the butler answered shortly in the negative; it was the prince's younger brother, Captain Stephen Saradine, he said. And with that the old man seemed to dry up suddenly and lose all taste for conversation.

After lunch had tailed off with exquisite coffee and liqueurs, the guests were introduced to the garden, the library, and the housekeeper – a dark handsome lady, of no little majesty, and rather like a plutonic Madonna. It appeared that she and the butler were the only survivors of the prince's original foreign ménage, all the other servants now in the house being new and collected in

Norfolk by the housekeeper. This latter lady went by the name of Mrs Anthony, but she spoke with a slight Italian accent, and Flambeau did not doubt that Anthony was a Norfolk version of some more Latin name. Mr Paul, the butler, also had a faintly foreign air, but he was in tongue and training English, as are many of the most polished men-servants of the cosmopolitan nobility.

Pretty and unique as it was, the place had about it a curious luminous sadness. Hours passed in it like days. The long, well-windowed rooms were full of daylight, but it seemed a dead daylight. And through all other incidental noises, the sound of talk, the clink of glasses, or the passing feet of servants, they could hear on all sides of the house the melancholy noise of the river.

'We have taken a wrong turning and come to a wrong place,' said Father Brown, looking out of the window at the grey-green sedges and the silver flood. 'Never mind; one can sometimes do good by being the right person in the wrong place.'

Father Brown, though commonly a silent, was an oddly sympathetic little man, and in those few but endless hours he unconsciously sank deeper into the secrets of Reed House than his professional friend. He had that knack of friendly silence which is so essential to gossip; and saying scarcely a word, he probably obtained from his new acquaintances all that in any case they would have told. The butler indeed was naturally uncommunicative. He betrayed a sullen and almost animal affection for his master, who, he said, had been very badly treated. The chief offender seemed to be his highness's brother, whose name alone would lengthen the old man's lantern jaws and pucker his parrot nose into a sneer. Captain Stephen was a ne'er-do-well, apparently, and had drained his benevolent brother of hundreds and thousands; forced him to fly from fashionable life and live quietly in this retreat. That was all Paul, the butler, would say, and Paul was obviously a partisan.

The Italian housekeeper was somewhat more communicative, being, as Brown fancied, somewhat less content. Her tone about her master was faintly acid, though not without a certain awe. Flambeau and his friend were standing in the room of the looking-glasses examining the red sketch of the two boys when the housekeeper swept in swiftly on some domestic errand. It was a peculiarity of this glittering, glass-panelled place that anyone entering was reflected in four or five mirrors at once; and Father Brown, without turning round, stopped in the middle of a sentence of family criticism. But Flambeau, who had his face close up to the picture, was already saying in a loud voice: 'The brothers Saradine, I suppose. They both look innocent enough. It would be hard to say which is the good brother and which the bad.' Then realizing the lady's presence, he turned the conversation with some triviality, and strolled out into the garden. But Father Brown still gazed steadily at the red crayon sketch; and Mrs Anthony still gazed steadily at Father Brown.

She had large and tragic brown eyes, and her olive face glowed darkly with a curious and painful wonder – as of one doubtful of a stranger's identity or purpose. Whether the little priest's coat and creed touched some southern memories of confession, or whether she fancied he knew more than he did, she said to him in a low voice, as to a fellow plotter: 'He is right enough in one way, your friend. He says it would be hard to pick out the good and bad brothers. Oh, it would be hard, it would be mighty hard, to pick out the good one.'

'I don't understand you,' said Father Brown, and began to move away.

The woman took a step nearer to him, with thunderous brows and a sort of savage stoop, like a bull lowering his horns.

'There isn't a good one,' she hissed. 'There was badness enough in the captain taking all that money, but I don't think there was much goodness in the prince giving it. The captain's not the only man with something against him.'

A light dawned on the cleric's averted face, and his mouth formed silently the word 'blackmail'. Even as he did so the woman turned an abrupt white face over her shoulder and almost fell. The door had opened soundlessly and the pale Paul stood like a ghost in the doorway. By the weird trick of the reflecting walls, it seemed as if five Pauls had entered by five doors simultaneously.

'His Highness,' he said, 'has just arrived.'

In the same flash the figure of a man had passed outside the first window, crossing the sunlit pane like a lighted stage. An instant later he passed at the second window, and the many mirrors repainted in successive frames the same eagle profile and marching figure. He was erect and alert, but his hair was white and his complexion of an odd ivory yellow. He had that short, curved Roman nose which generally goes with long, lean cheeks and chin, but these were partly masked by moustache and imperial. The moustache was much darker than the beard, giving an effect slightly theatrical, and he was dressed up to the same dashing part, having a white top hat, an orchid in his coat, a yellow waistcoat and yellow gloves which he flapped and swung as he walked. When he came round to the front door they heard the stiff Paul open it, and heard the new arrival say cheerfully: 'Well, you see I have come.' The stiff Mr Paul bowed and answered in his inaudible manner; for a few minutes their conversation could not be heard. Then the butler said: 'Everything is at your disposal'; and the glove-flapping Prince Saradine came gaily into the room to greet them. They beheld once more that spectral scene – five princes entering a room with five doors.

The prince put the white hat and yellow gloves on the table and offered his hand quite cordially.

'Delighted to see you here, Mr Flambeau,' he said. 'Know you very well by reputation, if that's not an indiscreet remark.'

'Not at all,' answered Flambeau, laughing. 'I am not sensitive. Very few reputations are gained by unsullied virtue.'

The prince flashed a sharp look at him to see if the retort had any personal point; then he laughed also and offered chairs to everyone, including himself.

'Pleasant little place this, I think,' he said with a detached air. 'Not much to do, I fear; but the fishing is really good.'

The priest, who was staring at him with the grave stare of a baby, was haunted by some fancy that escaped definition. He looked at the grey, carefully curled hair, yellow-white visage, and slim, somewhat foppish figure. These were not unnatural, though perhaps a shade *prononcé*, like the outfit of a figure behind the footlights. The nameless interest lay in something else, in the very framework of the face; Brown was tormented with a half memory of having seen it somewhere before. The man looked like some old friend of his dressed up. Then he remembered the mirrors, and put his fancy down to some psychological effect of that multiplication of human masks.

Prince Saradine distributed his social attentions between his guests with great gaiety and tact. Finding the detective of a sporting turn and eager to employ his holiday, he guided Flambeau and Flambeau's boat down to the best fishing spot in the stream, and was back in his own canoe in twenty minutes to join Father Brown in the library and plunge equally politely into the priest's more philosophic pleasures. He seemed to know a great deal both about the fishing and the books, though of these not the most edifying; he spoke five or six languages, though chiefly the slang of each. He had evidently lived in varied cities and very motley societies, for some of his cheerfullest stories were about gambling hells and opium dens, Australian bushrangers or Italian brigands. Father Brown knew that the once celebrated Saradine had spent his last few years in almost ceaseless travel, but he had not guessed that the travels were so disreputable or so amusing.

Indeed, with all his dignity of a man of the world, Prince Saradine radiated, to such sensitive observers as the priest, a certain atmosphere of the restless and even the unreliable. His face was fastidious, but his eye was wild; he had little nervous tricks, like a man shaken by drink or drugs; and he neither had, nor professed to have, his hand on the helm of household affairs. All these were left to the two old servants, especially to the butler, who was plainly the central pillar of the house. Mr Paul, indeed, was not so much a butler as a sort of steward, or even chamberlain; he dined privately, but with almost as much pomp as his master; he was feared by all the servants; and he consulted with the prince decorously, but somewhat unbendingly – rather as if he were the prince's solicitor. The sombre housekeeper was a mere shadow in comparison; indeed, she seemed to efface herself and wait only on the butler, and Brown heard no more of those volcanic whispers which had half told him of the younger brother who blackmailed the elder. Whether the prince was really being thus bled by the absent captain he could not be certain, but there was something insecure and secretive about Saradine that made the tale by no means incredible.

When they went once more into the long hall with the windows and the mirrors yellow evening was dropping over the waters and the willowy banks, and a bittern sounded in the distance like an elf upon his dwarfish drum. The same singular sentiment of some sad and evil fairyland crossed the priest's mind again like a grey cloud. 'I wish Flambeau were back,' he muttered.

'Do you believe in doom?' asked the restless Prince Saradine suddenly.

'No,' answered his guest. 'I believe in Doomsday.'

The prince turned from the window and stared at him in a singular manner, his face in shadow against the sunset. 'What do you mean?' he asked.

'I mean that we here are on the wrong side of the tapestry,' answered Father Brown. 'The things that happen here do not seem to mean anything; they mean something somewhere else. Somewhere else retribution will come on the real offender. Here it often seems to fall on the wrong person.'

The prince made an inexplicable noise like an animal; in his shadowed face the eyes were shining queerly. A new and shrewd thought exploded silently in the other's mind. Was there another meaning in Saradine's blend of brilliancy and abruptness? Was the prince – Was he perfectly sane? He was repeating, 'The wrong person – the wrong person,' many more times than was natural in a social exclamation.

Then Father Brown awoke tardily to a second truth. In the mirrors before him he could see the silent door standing open, and the silent Mr Paul standing in it, with his usual pallid impassiveness.

'I thought it better to announce at once,' he said, with the same stiff respectfulness as of an old family lawyer, 'a boat rowed by six men has come to the landing-stage, and there's a gentleman sitting in the stern.'

'A boat!' repeated the prince; 'a gentleman?' and he rose to his feet.

There was a startled silence punctuated only by the odd noise of the bird in the sedge; and then, before anyone could speak again, a new face and figure passed in profile round the three sunlit windows, as the prince had passed an hour or two before. But except for the accident that both outlines were aquiline, they had little in common. Instead of the new white topper of Saradine, was a black one of antiquated or foreign shape; under it was a young and very solemn face, clean shaven, blue about its resolute chin, and carrying a faint suggestion of the young Napoleon. The association was assisted by something old and odd about the whole get-up, as of a man who had never troubled to change the fashions of his fathers. He had a shabby blue frock-coat, a red, soldierly-looking waistcoat, and a kind of coarse white trousers common among the early Victorians, but strangely incongruous today. From all this old clothes-shop his olive face stood out strangely young and monstrously sincere.

'The deuce!' said Prince Saradine, and clapping on his white hat he went to the front door himself, flinging it open on the sunset garden.

By that time the newcomer and his followers were drawn up on the lawn like a small stage army. The six boatmen had pulled the boat well up on shore, and were guarding it almost menacingly holding their oars erect like spears. They were swarthy men, and some of them wore earrings. But one of them stood forward beside the olive-faced young man in the red waistcoat, and carried a large black case of unfamiliar form.

'Your name,' said the young man, 'is Saradine?'

Saradine assented rather negligently.

The newcomer had dull, dog-like brown eyes, as different as possible from the restless and glittering grey eyes of the prince. But once again Father Brown was tortured with a sense of having seen somewhere a replica of the face; and once again he remembered the repetitions of the glass-panelled room, and put down the coincidence to that. 'Confound this crystal palace!' he muttered. 'One sees everything too many times. It's like a dream.'

'If you are Prince Saradine,' said the young man, 'I may tell you that my name is Antonelli.'

'Antonelli,' repeated the prince languidly. 'Somehow I remember the name.'

'Permit me to present myself,' said the young Italian.

With his left hand he politely took off his old-fashioned top hat; with his right he caught Prince Saradine so ringing a crack across the face that the white top hat rolled down the steps and one of the blue flowerpots rocked upon its pedestal.

The prince, whatever he was, was evidently not a coward; he sprang at his enemy's throat and almost bore him backwards to the grass. But his enemy extricated himself with a singularly inappropriate air of hurried politeness.

'That is all right,' he said, panting and in halting English. 'I have insulted. I will give satisfaction. Marco, open the case.'

The man beside him with the earrings and the big black case proceeded to unlock it. He took out of it two long Italian rapiers, with splendid steel hilts and blades, which he planted point downwards in the lawn. The strange young man standing facing the entrance with his yellow and vindictive face, the two swords standing up in the turf like two crosses in a cemetery, and the line of the ranked rowers behind, gave it all an odd appearance of being some barbaric court of justice. But everything else was unchanged, so sudden had been the interruption. The sunset gold still glowed on the lawn, and the bittern still boomed as if announcing some small but dreadful destiny.

'Prince Saradine,' said the man called Antonelli; 'when I was an infant in the cradle you killed my father and stole my mother; my father was the more fortunate. You did not kill him fairly, as I am going to kill you. You and my wicked mother took him driving to a lonely pass in Sicily, flung him down a cliff, and went on your way. I could imitate you if I chose, but imitating you is too vile. I have followed you all over the world, and you have always fled from me. But this is the end of the world – and of you. I have you now, and I give you the chance you never gave my father. Choose one of those swords.'

Prince Saradine, with contracted brows, seemed to hesitate a moment, but his ears were still singing with the blow, and he sprang forward and snatched at one of the hilts. Father Brown had also sprung forward, striving to compose the dispute; but he soon found his personal presence made matters worse. Saradine was a French Freemason and a fierce atheist, and a priest moved him by the law of contraries. And for the other man neither priest nor layman moved him at all. This young man with the Bonaparte face and the brown eyes was something far sterner than a puritan – a pagan. He was a simple slayer from the morning of the earth; a man of the stone age – a man of stone.

One hope remained, the summoning of the household; and Father Brown ran back into the house. He found, however, that all the underservants had been given a holiday ashore by the autocrat Paul, and that only the sombre Mrs Anthony moved uneasily about the long rooms. But the moment she turned a ghastly face upon him, he resolved one of the riddles of the house of mirrors. The heavy brown eyes of Antonelli were the heavy brown eyes of Mrs Anthony, and in a flash he saw half the story.

'Your son is outside,' he said, without wasting words;

'either he or the prince will be killed. Where is Mr Paul?'

'He is at the landing-stage,' said the woman faintly. 'He is – he is – signalling for help.'

'Mrs Anthony,' said Father Brown seriously, 'there is no time for nonsense. My friend has his boat down the river, fishing. Your son's boat is guarded by your son's men. There is only this one canoe; what is Mr Paul doing with it?'

'Santa Maria! I do not know,' she said; and swooned all her length on the matted floor.

Father Brown lifted her to a sofa, flung a pot of water over her, shouted for help, and then rushed down to the landing-stage of the little island. But the canoe was already in mid-stream, and old Paul was pulling and pushing it up the river with an energy incredible at his years.

'I will save my master,' he cried, his eyes blazing maniacally. 'I will save him yet!'

Father Brown could do nothing but gaze after the boat as it struggled upstream, and pray that the old man might waken the little town in time.

'A duel is bad enough,' he muttered, rubbing up his rough dust-coloured hair, 'but there's something wrong about this duel, even as a duel. I feel it in my bones. But what can it be?'

As he stood staring at the water, a wavering mirror of sunset, he heard from the other end of the island garden a small but unmistakable sound – the cold concussion of steel. He turned his head.

Away on the farthest cape or headland of the long islet, on a strip of turf beyond the last rank of roses, the duellists had already crossed swords. Evening above them was a dome of virgin gold, and, distant as they were, every detail was picked out. They had cast off their coats, but the yellow waistcoat and white hair of Saradine, the red waistcoat and white trousers of Antonelli, glittered in the level light like the colours of the dancing clockwork dolls. The two swords sparkled from point to pommel like two diamond pins. There was something frightful in the two figures appearing so little and so gay. They looked like two butterflies trying to pin each other to a cork.

Father Brown ran as hard as he could, his little legs going like a wheel. But when he came to the field of combat he found he was both too late and too early – too late to stop the strife, under the shadow of the grim Sicilians leaning on their oars, and too early to anticipate any disastrous issue of it. For the two men were singularly well matched, the prince using his skill with a sort of cynical confidence, the Sicilian using his with a murderous care. Few finer fencing matches can ever have been seen in crowded amphitheatres than that which tinkled and sparkled on that forgotten island in the reedy river. The dizzy fight was balanced so long that hope began to revive in the protesting priest; by all common probability Paul must soon come back with the police. It would be some comfort even if Flambeau came back from his fishing, for Flambeau, physically speaking, was worth four other men. But there was no sign of Flambeau, and, what was much queerer, no sign of Paul or the police. No other raft or stick was left to float on; in that lost island in that vast nameless pool, they were cut off as on a rock in the Pacific.

Almost as he had the thought the ringing of the rapiers

quickened to a rattle, the prince's arms flew up, and the point shot out behind between his shoulder-blades. He went over with a great whirling movement, almost like one throwing the half of a boy's cart-wheel. The sword flew from his hand like a shooting star, and dived into the distant river; and he himself sank with so earth-shaking a subsidence that he broke a big rose-tree with his body and shook up into the sky a cloud of red earth – like the smoke of some heathen sacrifice. The Sicilian had made blood-offering to the ghost of his father.

The priest was instantly on his knees by the corpse, but only to make too sure that it was a corpse. As he was still trying some last hopeless tests he heard for the first time voices from farther up the river, and saw a police-boat shoot up to the landing-stage with constables and other important people, including the excited Paul. The little priest rose with a distinctly dubious grimace.

'Now, why on earth,' he muttered, 'why on earth couldn't he have come before?'

Some seven minutes later the island was occupied by an invasion of townsfolk and police, and the latter had put their hands on the victorious duellist, ritually re-minding him that anything he said might be used against him.

'I shall not say anything,' said the monomaniac, with a wonderful and peaceful face. 'I shall never say anything any more. I am very happy, and I only want to be hanged.'

Then he shut his mouth as they led him away, and it is the strange but certain truth that he never opened it again in this world, except to say 'Guilty' at his trial.

Father Brown had stared at the suddenly crowded

garden, the arrest of the man of blood, the carrying away of the corpse after its examination by the doctor, rather as one watches the break-up of some ugly dream; he was motionless, like a man in a nightmare. He gave his name and address as a witness, but declined their offer of a boat to the shore, and remained alone in the island garden, gazing at the broken rose bush and the whole green theatre of that swift and inexplicable tragedy. The light died along the river; mist rose in the marshy banks; a few belated birds flitted fitfully across.

Stuck stubbornly in his sub-consciousness (which was an unusually lively one) was an unspeakable certainty that there was something still unexplained. This sense that had clung to him all day could not be fully explained by his fancy about 'looking-glass land'. Somehow he had not seen the real story, but some game or masque. And yet people do not get hanged or run through the body for the sake of a charade.

As he sat on the steps of the landing-stage ruminating he grew conscious of the tall, dark streak of a sail coming silently down the shining river, and sprang to his feet with such a back-rush of feeling that he almost wept.

'Flambeau!' he cried, and shook his friend by both hands again and again, much to the astonishment of that sportsman, as he came on shore with his fishing tackle. 'Flambeau,' he said, 'so you're not killed?'

'Killed!' repeated the angler in great astonishment. 'And why should I be killed?'

'Oh, because nearly everybody else is,' said his companion rather wildly. 'Saradine got murdered, and Antonelli wants to be hanged, and his mother's fainted, and I, for one, don't know whether I'm in this world or the next. But, thank God, you're in the same one.' And he took the bewildered Flambeau's arm.

As they turned from the landing-stage they came under the eaves of the low bamboo house and looked in through one of the windows, as they had done on their first arrival. They beheld a lamp-lit interior well calculated to arrest their eyes. The table in the long dining-room had been laid for dinner when Saradine's destroyer had fallen like a storm-bolt on the island. And the dinner was now in placid progress, for Mrs Anthony sat somewhat sullenly at the foot of the table, while at the head of it was Mr Paul, the major-domo: eating and drinking of the best, his bleared, bluish eyes standing queerly out of his face, his gaunt countenance inscrutable, but by no means devoid of satisfaction.

With a gesture of powerful impatience, Flambeau rattled at the window, wrenched it open, and put an indignant head into the lamp-lit room.

'Well!' he cried; 'I can understand you may need some refreshment, but really to steal your master's dinner while he lies murdered in the garden –'

'I have stolen a great many things in a long and pleasant life,' replied the strange old gentleman placidly; 'this dinner is one of the few things I have not stolen. This dinner and this house and garden happen to belong to me.'

A thought flashed across Flambeau's face. 'You mean to say,' he began, 'that the will of Prince Saradine –'

'I am Prince Saradine,' said the old man, munching a salted almond.

Father Brown, who was looking at the birds outside,

jumped as if he were shot, and put in at the window a pale face like a turnip.

'You are *what*?' he repeated in a shrill voice.

'Paul Prince Saradine, *à vos ordres*,' said the venerable person politely, lifting a glass of sherry. 'I live here very quietly, being a domestic kind of fellow; and for the sake of modesty I am called Mr Paul, to distinguish me from my unfortunate brother Mr Stephen. He died, I hear, recently – in the garden. Of course, it is not my fault if enemies pursue him to this place. It is owing to the regrettable irregularity of his life. He was not a domestic character.'

He relapsed into silence, and continued to gaze at the opposite wall just above the bowed and sombre head of the woman. They saw plainly the family likeness that had haunted them in the dead man. Then his old shoulders began to heave and shake a little, as if he were choking, but his face did not alter.

'My God!' cried Flambeau after a pause; 'he's laughing!'

'Come away,' said Father Brown, who was quite white. 'Come away from this house of hell. Let us get into an honest boat again.'

Night had sunk on rushes and river by the time they had pushed off from the island, and they went downstream in the dark, warming themselves with two big cigars that glowed like crimson ships' lanterns. Father Brown took his cigar out of his mouth and said:

'I suppose you can guess the whole story now? After all, it's a primitive story. A man had two enemies. He was a wise man. And so he discovered that two enemies are better than one.'

'I do not follow that,' answered Flambeau.

'Oh, it's really simple,' rejoined his friend. 'Simple, though anything but innocent. Both the Saradines were scamps: but the prince, the elder, was the sort of scamp that gets to the top; and the younger, the captain, was the sort that sinks to the bottom. This squalid officer fell from beggar to blackmailer, and one ugly day he got his hold upon his brother the prince. Obviously it was for no light matter, for Prince Paul Saradine was frankly "fast", and had no reputation to lose as to the mere sins of society. In plain fact, it was a hanging matter, and Stephen literally had a rope round his brother's neck. He had somehow discovered the truth about the Sicilian affair, and could prove that Paul murdered old Antonelli in the mountains. The captain raked in the hush money heavily for ten years, until even the prince's splendid fortune began to look a little foolish.

'But Prince Saradine bore another burden besides his blood-sucking brother. He knew that the son of Antonelli, a mere child at the time of the murder, had been trained in savage Sicilian loyalty, and lived only to avenge his father, not with the gibbet (for he lacked Stephen's legal proof), but with the old weapons of vendetta. The boy had practised arms with a deadly perfection, and about the time that he was old enough to use them Prince Saradine began, as the society papers said, to travel. The fact is that he began to flee for his life, passing from place to place like a hunted criminal; but with one relentless man upon his trail. That was Prince Paul's position, and by no means a pretty one. The more money he spent on eluding Antonelli the less he had to silence Stephen. The more he gave to silence Stephen the less chance there was of finally escaping Antonelli. Then it was that he showed himself a great man – a genius like Napoleon.

'Instead of resisting his two antagonists, he surrendered suddenly to both of them. He gave way, like a Japanese wrestler, and his foes fell prostrate before him. He gave up the race round the world, and he gave up his address to young Antonelli; then he gave up everything to his brother. He sent Stephen money enough for smart clothes and easy travel, with a letter saying roughly: 'This is all I have left. You have cleaned me out. I still have a little house in Norfolk, with servants and a cellar, and if you want more from me you must take that. Come and take possession if you like, and I will live there quietly as your friend or agent or anything.' He knew that the Sicilian had never seen the Saradine brothers save, perhaps, in pictures; he knew they were somewhat alike, both having grey, pointed beards. Then he shaved his own face and waited. The trap worked. The unhappy captain, in his new clothes, entered the house in triumph as a prince, and walked upon the Sicilian's sword.

'There was one hitch, and it is to the honour of human nature. Evil spirits like Saradine often blunder by never expecting the virtues of mankind. He took it for granted that the Italian's blow, when it came, would be dark, violent and nameless, like the blow it avenged; that the victim would be knifed at night, or shot from behind a hedge, and so die without speech. It was a bad minute for Prince Paul when Antonelli's chivalry proposed a formal duel, with all its possible explanations. It was then that I found him putting off in his boat with wild eyes. He was fleeing, bareheaded, in an open boat before Antonelli should learn who he was.

'But, however agitated, he was not hopeless. He knew the adventurer and he knew the fanatic. It was quite probable that Stephen, the adventurer, would hold his tongue, through his mere histrionic pleasure in playing a part, his lust for clinging to his new cosy quarters, his rascal's trust in luck, and his fine fencing. It was certain that Antonelli, the fanatic, would hold his tongue, and be hanged without telling tales of his family. Paul hung about on the river till he knew the fight was over. Then he roused the town, brought police, saw his two vanquished enemies taken away for ever, and sat down smiling to his dinner.'

'Laughing, God help us!' said Flambeau with a strong shudder. 'Do they get such ideas from Satan?'

'He's got that idea from you,' answered the priest.

'God forbid!' ejaculated Flambeau. 'From me? What do you mean?'

The priest pulled a visiting-card from his pocket and held it up in the faint glow of his cigar; it was scrawled with green ink.

'Don't you remember his original invitation to you?' he asked; 'and the compliment to your criminal exploit? "That trick of yours," he says, "of getting one detective to arrest the other?" He has just copied your trick. With an enemy on each side of him he slipped swiftly out of the way and let them collide and kill each other.'

Flambeau tore Prince Saradine's card from the priest's hands and rent it savagely in small pieces.

'There's the last of that old skull and crossbones,' he said as he scattered the pieces upon the dark and disappearing waves of the stream; 'but I should think it would poison the fishes.'

The last gleam of white card and green ink was drowned and darkened; a faint and vibrant colour as of morning changed the sky, and the moon behind the grasses grew paler. They drifted in silence.

'Father,' said Flambeau suddenly, 'do you think it was all a dream?'

The priest shook his head, whether in dissent or agnosticism, but remained mute. A smell of hawthorn and of orchards came to them through the darkness, telling them that a wind was awake; the next moment it swayed their little boat and swelled their sail, and carried them onward down the winding river to happier places and the homes of harmless men.